By: S.J. Mitch

Published by Written Creativity LLC

Artwork By Craiyon

Table of Contents

Prologue

When I decided to move to the busy city of Atlanta, I thought things would start looking up for me. I was wrong. My name is Janice Allen. I'm a twenty-seven-year-old lesbian who recently moved to Atlanta for a fresh start. Some say Atlanta is the place where a young lesbian with a construction business degree can become successful.

I've been here for a year now. My ex-wife and I divorced nine months ago, and I've tried to live my best life ever since. I'm a pretty good catch. I have my own business, live in a beautiful loft apartment in the middle of Buckhead overseeing downtown Atlanta, and am not a bad-looking lesbian.

Coming from a small town in Alabama, I always dreamed of starting my own construction company, so that was my plan after graduation.

Fortunately, nothing was left for me in my small hometown after my divorce. So, the same day my divorce was final, my best friend and I packed up an extra-large U-Haul and headed to Georgia.

A few months after moving to Atlanta, I met this woman, Elle. She was beautiful, intelligent, and everything I was looking for, coming out of a toxic marriage. We would go to the movies and eat junk food while watching two or three films. On our off days, we would lie in bed and talk for hours until we fell asleep wrapped in each other arms. She would listen to each word with amazement when I spoke of my day. I would tell her stories about my toxic ex-marriage, and she would rub her fingers through my hair, relaxing me with each touch. Then, she would pull my hair back and kiss my forehead to bring me back to reality.

Sometimes, I would come home from a long job, tired and exhausted, and she would come over, cook me dinner, and then lie in bed listening to old-school music in the dark. I miss those days. She was my escape those days, and now she brings on more drama than the world around me.

Chapter One

I woke up next to Elle, still sleeping. I didn't want to wake her because I knew she was still upset about our previous argument. We had just come from dinner when my phone began going off. It was an unknown call, so I didn't answer them and kept sending them to voicemail. I forgot to stop my work phone from forwarding it to my personal phone. Elle insisted that I answer the phone, which turned into an argument about me hiding things and sneaking around. I was too tired from working all day to explain to her or a potential customer that I don't answer phone calls after working hours. So I ignored them both and went to bed.

If it weren't for the fact that it was after one in the morning, I would have gone to my own home. But I had a few drinks over dinner, so I passed out when we returned to Elle's place. It was now eight in the morning, and I wanted to get out of there as quickly as possible before we picked up where we had left off.

I rolled over and retrieved my cell phone from my pants pocket on the floor. After realizing that I didn't get a chance to charge it, I immediately checked the battery percentage. I had a little less than half and wasn't happy about that. I pulled down the notification bar and glanced at my text messages:

Mya: I just landed in Atlanta.

Damn really? I thought as I read the preview notification in my status bar. Instead of replying, I locked my phone and sat it on the nightstand. I sat up slowly, trying not to move too much and wake Elle.

I scooted over to the edge of the bed and felt her move. I looked behind me and saw her staring. Neither of us said a word as I grabbed my jeans and headed to the bathroom. I closed the door behind me and glanced at my reflection. I grabbed my toothbrush and stood there, eyeing my 5'10, 160-pound frame, trying to figure out how to leave this woman's condo without starting an argument. As I turned on the water, Elle entered the bathroom and quickly sat on the toilet.

"Good morning!" I said. There was no answer as she began to relieve herself. I brushed my teeth, rinsed my mouth, and slid on my jeans. I walked out just before she washed her hands. I grabbed my shirt off the floor and slipped it over my head.

"I'll call you later," I said, grabbing my phone and keys off the nightstand.

"I thought it was going to be you and me today? I guess you changed your mind," she responded quickly.

"I need some space. Last night was a lot," I said.

"It was a lot because you're still hiding your phone," she said.

"I'm hiding my phone because I didn't want to answer the call. Come on," I said.

"Then tell me who it is," Elle said as she sat on the bed and folded her arms.

I unlocked my phone and showed her the two unknown missed calls from last night.

"I don't know who it is, Elle. You know my phone is connected to the website right now. I don't answer after hours," I said and snatched my phone from her face. I was so tired of the back-and-forth arguing and bickering. I grabbed the rest of my things.

"Whatever," she said.

"Let me go and handle some things, and I'll call you later. We can meet back up tonight," I told Elle. She sucked her teeth as she sat down on the bed. I walked over and tried to give her a half kiss on the forehead, but she turned her head before my lips could make contact, climbed back into bed, and grabbed her phone.

"Yeah, okay," she said. Once Elle had decided that she was upset, there was nothing I could have said or done. These arguments were becoming daily, and I was exhausted trying to figure out what to say or not to say when we were around each other.

I made a mental note to check her Twitter page because I knew she would tweet about everything, as always. I could check her page to see what was on her mind. She wouldn't say anything to me but blast it all over social media. Lately, things have gotten so bad that I deleted her from all my social media and blocked her from some. I got tired of seeing all the negative things and posts. Elle was forty-three and could act seventeen sometimes.

Without saying goodbye, I headed for the door. After locking Elle's front door with my spare key that I've had since a month after our talking, I unlocked my phone and read my messages. She didn't have a key to my place, though. I didn't see a reason to give her one. We stopped going to my place months ago. I would instead come to hers. It was easier for me to leave. I clicked on the notification and began to text Mya back.

I asked Mya if I could see her today, and she immediately texted back with her address. She was staying at the Downtown Westin, and that made me happy because she wasn't too far. Your location in

Atlanta is crucial because a two-mile drive could turn into a thirty-minute drive, depending on your location. After living downtown for almost a year, it was the only part of town I knew my way through, along with all the back roads. I texted her back and told her I would arrive in a few hours.

I started my 2011 Range Rover, plugged my phone into the jack, and turned on Pandora. I put my truck in drive and pulled off. I needed to get home, shower, and change my clothes. It was my first day off in about a week, and I wanted to enjoy it. Spending it with Elle was not an option. We can argue later.

I pulled to my apartment, exited the car, and headed to the elevator. I pushed the button to the sixth floor. As I exited the elevator, I saw Tammy coming out of her apartment, holding a trash bag, wearing her usual workout tights and sports bra. "Hey, Tammy! What I told you about taking the trash out dressed like that, you know I'm looking." I joked.

"Girl, stop it before I call your girl. You know she already doesn't like me," she responded before dropping her trash down the garbage shoot. She was right. Elle didn't like any girl who smiled or looked my way, even though Tammy was straight and married with kids.

"I'm just saying. You're the one walking out here like that," I said.

"I just came from yoga, and what will you do with this? You can't handle a real "boriqua," Tammy said in her deep accent. She tossed her trash into the chute. Instead of answering, I stood at the door and smiled. "Exactly."

Don't get me wrong. I've thought about it when I first moved into my place. Tammy was the first person to introduce themselves to me. I was on the last of three trips from the back of my car to my apartment with a buggy full of boxes. I didn't have much. My college dorm was only so big.

I was fresh out of college, and it was my first place. I was too excited to move into the building. At the time, I was staying in a hotel and had been for the past month or so and couldn't wait to get the keys.

Tammy held the elevator open for me as I dragged the buggy across the courtyard.

"Sixth floor," I said.

"Same as me. Hello, neighbor," she said.

She let me off the elevator first and walked behind me as I pushed the last of my belongings.

"Are you following me, or do you live this way?" I said, reaching my door.

"Funny! I actually live right here, smart ass," she said.

"Well, hello, neighbor," I said. We both laughed and disappeared into our places. From that moment forward, she was my favorite neighbor. When I first arrived and didn't know anyone, she invited me to the bar a few times and even brought me breakfast a few times when she knew I was sick.

Tammy was just a spoiled housewife of a pilot. He was rarely home, and I may have met him twice. She did have two little boys, maybe six and seven. I was convinced he had a second family somewhere. She would joke about it, but I knew there was some truth in there somewhere. Tammy and the boys spent most of their time in the courtyard on the roof. It was the hangout spot for residences with a lounge, pool, foosball tables, and a heated pool overlooking Downtown Atlanta.

I used to take Elle there a lot when we started hanging out, but eventually stopped. Elle would see her and her kids and insist it was something between us, even calling herself and confronting her once.

We had just come from the movies. The theater is where you can order food and drinks in the movies. I had never been and never heard of anything like it. The only movie theater I had in my small town didn't even show IMAX or 3D movies. You have to drive to Montgomery for that.

After the movie, Elle was a little drunk. I was sober as hell. It was a long work day that day, and I knew if I had any alcohol, I would have been asleep. So, I ordered her food and drinks and got myself a lemonade with my meal. Elle had been asking to go to the movies for weeks, and although I was tired, I wanted to keep my promise.

Anyway, Elle and I were walking down the hallway to my door when Tammy came out of her apartment holding a small trash bag. I smiled and spoke to Tammy as I normally had done daily for the three months I had lived there. Elle had only met a few weeks earlier. I let go of Elle's hand and reached into my pocket for my keys. When Tammy had passed us, Elle stopped walking and looked at me with her hands on hips.

"So, you let go of my hand when she walked by?" Elle said, pointing simultaneously at us both.

"What are you talking about? I grabbed my keys," I said, dangling them in front of Elle. Tammy laughed and tossed her trash in the chute.

"You think this is funny?" Elle screamed at Tammy

"J, get your girl," Tammy said. I quickly unlocked the door and pulled Elle into the apartment before she could say anything else.

"What are you doing, Elle? You're drunk. Come on, let's get in bed," I said as I locked the door behind her. I grabbed Elle's hand and led her to my bedroom.

"I'm not stupid, and I know what's up," Elle slurred. She kicked off her shoes and threw herself across the bed. Elle was asleep within two minutes. That was her first negative encounter with Tammy, but it wouldn't be the last. Elle gave Tammy eye rolls every time she would see her.

Tammy was straight as an arrow. She might flirt here and there, but it was all harmless. She was a cool person, beautiful as hell. A "boricua," as she loves to say, who didn't look more than twenty-five, let alone forty-two with two kids.

Tammy curved her man and women in the building and made it known she was married. Trust me, most of them tried. Elle didn't like her because she said she always hung around the building with no clothes on. I would call it workout tights and a sports bra, no clothes, but she did have a banging body. Elle couldn't stand her either and would make comments about her seeking attention.

"It's not that I don't know what to do with it. You're just not ready to handle what needs to be done, smart ass," I said. Tammy had closed the trash chute and was headed back to her apartment.

"If I liked your girl, I would tell her about you, but let's be real," Tammy said in her deep accent. We both laughed. I unlocked my door and walked into my empty apartment.

"At this point, it's whatever," I said to myself. I locked the door behind me and threw my bag across my deserted sofa.

I've been spending the night at Elle's house so much last week that it felt weird being in my own apartment. But, on the other hand, being with her was better than sleeping alone. All I have are my thoughts when I'm alone, which I hate.

I kicked off my shoes, flopped on my three-piece black sectional, grabbed the remote, and flipped through the music channels. I stopped at the pop channel and cut the volume up.

I ripped off my clothes, grabbed my towel, and turned on the shower. After dancing in the mirror for a few minutes, I hopped in and let the water run down my back. I couldn't stop thinking about the first time I ran into Mya.

Chapter Two

Mya was this cutie I met while working at her mother's home. She was visiting her parents while I was rebuilding their new kitchen. From the first moment she opened the door, I was in awe. Her five-foot-six-inch frame and long hair that she always kept swept to one side caught me by surprise. She was standing at the door looking sexy as ever in pajama shorts and a spaghetti strap shirt that stopped right above her pierced belly button. She reminded me of Aaliyah with honey-brown eyes.

"We're from Mavis Interior Design, here to install your new kitchen," I stuttered, repeating the rehearsed line when greeting a new customer. It was our fourth job and our second large client since starting our business. We did some cabinetry work, but this was a complete redesign, and both my business partner and I were excited.

"Come on inside. My mother told me you guys were coming. She's at work. My name is Mya," she returned as she opened the door. She stepped to the side and escorted us to the kitchen. I could see Toni staring at her body from the corner of my eyes. I rolled my eyes, thinking to myself, this chick is always thinking about the next fuck. She pointed towards the kitchen and walked back upstairs. Halfway up the stairs, she turned around and told us to ask if we needed anything to yell. I told her okay and started to get to work.

"You think she saw me staring at her booty?" Toni asked as soon as she disappeared.

"I'm pretty sure she saw you, but she's not paying us any attention. Let's get to work. We have a tight time frame on this job," I told her, trying to get Mya's booty off her mind and into the job.

We were halfway done, around two in the afternoon, when Mya finally showed her gorgeous face and asked if we wanted anything to drink.

"No, we came prepared," I said with a smile, pointing to a small cooler we bring to each job. Toni and I usually keep the cooler filled with ice and cold water. Mya wiped a piece of hair out of her face and smiled back. We stood there for a second, staring at each other, when Toni interrupted us, saying that we still had much to do and needed to return to work.

"Yeah, let's get back to work. I'm trying to get out of here by six," I agreed, responding to Toni but still locking eyes with Mya.

"You sure you don't need anything?" she said, still not breaking contact.

"No, we're okay, but if we do, I'll make sure to call you," I said before finally breaking our stare and returning my attention to Toni. I could see the jealousy in Toni's eyes. I brushed it off with a slight smile and continued to work.

"Okay, make sure you do," she strolled away.

"I think she's feeling you. You should get her number," Toni said, but the tone of her voice told me that she was a little salty.

"Now you know I'm not checking for no females right now. Elle and I are doing good, and I want to keep it that way," I told Toni, but in the back of my head, I was praying Mya would come back down the stairs.

On the next and final day of the remodel, Mya kept finding a reason to come downstairs. She needed water, a phone changer, and then it was the number of the refrigerator. While Toni was being overly helpful, I continued to work but took notice of the smile she gave every time our eyes made contact.

Just as I was about to call Mya's cute self from upstairs to sign the necessary paperwork, the front door opened, and in walked her mother.

"Omg. This is nice," Mya's mom said.

"We're almost done. We have to clean up our mess," I said, gathering our tools.

"Take your time. Is my daughter upstairs?"

"Yes, ma'am. Whenever you are ready, my partner has some papers for you to sign," I said, grabbing my tools. I walked past her carrying my tools. Toni introduced herself and took over. While I was packing everything in the back of the pick-up truck, Mya walked up to the car.

"Hey," she said, making me sling my head around like a kid caught in the refrigerator sneaking a late-night snack. I dropped my hammer on my foot. "Oh, I'm sorry. Did I scare you?"

"A little, but thank God for steel-toe shoes," I joked, knocking the heel of my foot against the bed of our new model Ford F350 work truck.

"It's sporadic seeing two women doing what you guys do; I'm impressed," Mya said.

"Really? I guess you don't meet too many women in this field," I said with a smile. She smiled back.

"This may be weird, and I don't do this often, but I'm leaving tomorrow. I'll be back in a few months, and I was just wondering if we can exchange numbers," she asked.

"Exchange numbers?" I asked.

"Yeah, unless you're married already," she said, glaring at my ring finger.

"No ring, and I wouldn't mind that at all. I'm just a little caught off guard," I said.

"I've been trying to get you to see me, but you've been so into your work," she said.

"I wasn't sure. I guess I suck at flirting," I said.

"Here's my number. Text me anytime," Mya continued, handing me a folded piece of paper with her name and phone number scribbled.

"I will," I said.

"Hopefully soon."

At that time, Elle and I relationship was already running its course. It had been two days since we had seen each other. The last conversation was a text argument about how I would rather us spend time at her house than at mine. We were arguing so much I didn't want to bring that to my home. Plus, it was easier to leave if I was at her place, and I think Elle enjoyed kicking me out when she had enough of my bullshit.

Toni walked out the front door with Mya's mother, just a little behind. I hurried, put Mya's number in my pocket, jumped, and grabbed the other equipment.

After setting down the tools, I glanced back at Mya, standing next to her mother with a smile on her face. I smiled back at her, motioning that I would call her. She gave me a nod, letting me know that she understood. Then, I turned my attention back to Toni, explaining to Mya's mother about our 30-day warranty.

Mya's mom thanked us and told us how she loved the kitchen. I told her she was welcome and handed her our business card just in case she knew anyone else looking to renovate.

Besides the small decorations, the interior decorator would return the next day and add the show product. Overall, we did a banging job. I was confident our client would be happy with the results. We never had anything less than an excellent client review, and multiple companies highly recommended us.

I am not an interior designer; I'm more like the muscle for interior decorators. They give my company the layout, and Toni and I tear down the old and build the new. Toni is this stud I met while in college. Her real name is Tonisha, but we call her Toni for short. She's my best friend, business partner, and the only person besides my family that I have in my life.

Toni was a special person. And if you would see us together, you would wonder how we became friends. Toni is a very masculine stud compared to me. I was more on the softer side. But despite our differences, we've been grinding together since graduating college.

Anyway, from that day on, Mya and I texted every day. While I was working or wasn't around Elle, we would stay on the phone for hours, getting to know each other. My relationship had been so messed up, and we were barely talking. I had nothing but time to speak with Mya. Never kept that a secret. I didn't need to because our messages were never about being with each other, only about our day or letting off some steam. I appreciate the friendship that was building. Now, Mya was back in Atlanta on break from school.

Chapter Three

After being interrupted by the notification ringtone on my cell phone, I turned off the shower, wrapped the towel around me, and walked back to my room. I grabbed my cell phone off the bed to read the missed message from Toni, who invited me to hang out that night.

Toni loved to go to clubs and parties and basically everything about Atlanta's nightlife. I was mostly a homebody. I would go out with her sometimes, but that's after she begged me for days, and I ended up giving in just to shut her up. If not for Mya being in town, I might have taken her up on her offer to avoid Elle. I had no plans to chill with Toni or see her face. My mind was stuck on Mya.

I texted Tonie back to tell her I had plans. I would have told her exactly the plans, but I wanted to avoid hearing the questions and concerns about my relationship with Elle. Toni responded by calling me lame for not wanting to party with her. I would be that tonight and every night if that meant spending time with Mya.

One thing I could say about Toni is that I have the time of my life every time I go out with her. But unfortunately, it ended with me doing something I would regret the following day. For instance, the last time I went out with her, I got so drunk that I passed out in the bar parking lot, laid out in the front seat with a puddle of vomit outside the driver's door. It took me two days to get over that hangover.

I returned my phone to the bed, ignoring Toni's last comment. Then, after about an hour of slowly getting dressed and dancing around the house, I grabbed my keys, took one look in the mirror, grabbed a matching fitted baseball cap off the wall, and proceeded to the door. After months of texting and talking, I felt like a high school girl going on her first date.

Once I got into my truck, I called Mya and told her I was coming. After she gave me the room number, I hung up the phone and turned my music up. I pulled off as The Weeknd's new single glared through the speakers. I danced along to the melody of the beat and let his lyrics speak to my soul, comparing my life to his song Wicked Games.

After about ten minutes, I pulled up to the hotel, found a parking spot, and turned off the ignition. The music still played through the speakers as I sat in my truck and attempted to fix my clothes. The last time I saw her, I was dirty and smelly in my work uniform, so I wanted to make a good impression this time.

I checked myself in the rearview mirror, content with what I saw. I stepped out of the car and straightened my black Levi jeans and my pink and black polo collar shirt. I readjusted my fitted cap, pulled my curly, shoulder-length hair into the open part of the pink and black snapback, and proceeded to the hotel's entrance.

Once inside the hotel, I took the stairs rather than the elevator because I feared tight spaces. I wasn't about to risk my luck on an elevator by myself. I would have quickly jumped on if people were waiting, but I decided to take the stairs since no one was there. Besides, it was only three floors up.

Finally, I located her door and knocked lightly. I was nervous, and I secretly hoped no one would answer. After a few seconds, Mya opened the door, and it was like a beam of sunshine hit me in my eyes. She was beautiful, even more stunning than I remember. The sunlight from the window made her almond-brown skin look smooth and silky.

She wore a long sundress, so long it almost concealed her feet. The top was wrapped and tied around her neck. Her hair was down and pulled to one side with a flower clip on the other. She looked like a

Hawaiian queen. She smiled, and I immediately noticed the dimple on her left cheek. She was beautiful, and I was nervous as hell.

"About time you got here, come on in," she said as she stepped to the side. I walked past her, trying not to gawk at her beauty. Her two-bedroom suite looked like an apartment with a living room, a full kitchen, and a separate bedroom. I walked into the living room and sat on the couch.

"This is a nice room," I said, admiring the suite.

"Thanks. I'm here for three weeks, so I wanted something comfortable, and I needed a full kitchen because I love to cook."

"You look beautiful, by the way," I confessed.

"You do, too. Not many people can pull off pink, but I like it on you," she said and sat beside me.

"So, do you have anything you want to do today?" I asked. I scooted closer so that we were hip to hip.

"Yeah, I was thinking we could go over to Piedmont Park. It's beautiful outside, and I love being outdoors. We could walk around the park and get to know each other?" she asked while smiling.

"Yeah, that's fine, I've never been there. I'm always down to do something new," I confessed. I felt my phone vibrate in my pocket, but I ignored it. It could only be one of two people: Toni, with whom I already explained I had plans, or Elle. I had already taken the forwarding off my cellphone when I left Elle's house.

"You want anything to drink?" she asked and stood up,

"Yeah, water would be all right," I told her.

While she was in the kitchen, I used that time to see who was texting my phone. As I predicted, it was Elle:

Elle: I don't know what has gotten into you, but you know that I wanted to talk to you. Apparently, you had other things to do than spend ten minutes talking to me. I know we're not together, but you can't sit here and say that we're not living like we are. I deserve a little more respect than what you're giving me. But if this isn't where you want to be, stop wasting my time.

Me: I know you wanted to talk, but this is my first day off in over a week. I just needed to get away and spend some time with myself. I'll be there later today, and we can talk about

whatever you want to talk about, okay?
I'm sorry for falling asleep last night,
but I was tired. I'll be there around 8.

I was not about to get into a text argument with her, so I decided to respond and tell her exactly what she wanted to hear, even if it was a half-truth. I slid my phone back into my pocket just as Mya returned with two water bottles. She handed me one and sat back down. Feeling parched, I opened it and took a sip.

"Was that your girlfriend? I know an angry text when I hear one?" Mya asked while smiling. I didn't know what to say. Honestly, Elle was not my girlfriend. We had never made it official, but she was the only person I slept with daily. Plus, we haven't gone a day without seeing each other for the past six months. So, I decided to tell the truth.

"Is that your way of asking if I'm single?" I joked. "But to answer your question, yeah, and no. No, because it was never established, but it has been about six months." Usually, I would say no and leave it at that because we're not official. But Mya has always made me comfortable opening up to her, and I didn't want to lie.

"Six months? That is a long time of talking. Are you sure you haven't established anything? Does she know your relationship isn't exclusive?" Mya said.

"Oh, she knows. It's been a constant argument for months," I said.

"On her end or yours?" Mya asked.

"You're asking many questions for someone with a girl at school," I said.

"Had. It wasn't working out," she said with a smile. I took another sip of water.

"Interesting," was all I managed to say.

"Are you going to answer my question? You can tell me if I'm overstepping. I tend to do that with someone I like," Mya said.

"No, you're good. It's me. I don't want to make things any more serious than it is right now. I've been avoiding a lot of things when it comes to that relationship," I said.

"Sometimes we tend to hold on to things we know we need to let go," Mya said.

"Are you giving me advice or speaking from experience?" I asked.

"I've heard very little of your relationship. I can't comment on that. I am speaking from experience," she said.

"I wouldn't call it a relationship," I said.

"What do you call it?" Mya asked.

"A very dysfunctional situationship," I said.

"I hope things clear up," she said.

I pushed Elle out of my mind. I would deal with her tonight. Until then, I was going to enjoy my day with Mya. As Elle said, we weren't official, so technically, this isn't cheating. For about an hour, we sat and talked about our lives.

Mya was from Atlanta but left a year ago and lived in Gainesville, Florida, where she is in her last semester at the University of Florida. At seventeen, she came out to her parents, who accepted her immediately. However, she said they were too wrapped in their melodrama to care about her sexuality.

Mya loved photography and painting. She visits Piedmont Park every time she comes home. Sometimes, Mya said she would sit on a blanket alone and read, draw, or paint for hours. However, she admitted that she doesn't visit there often with guests.

Mya's dad had recently passed, and her mother was going through a tough time. She came back to find a place here in the city. She loved the park and wanted to find something close to Piedmont Park. The girl Mya talks to is crazy in love with her, but Mya can't love her because she's still scared of her past. She keeps her around because she hates being in Florida alone.

Mya's longest relationship of three years ended a little over a year ago. She said the ex-girlfriend joined the Air Force and wouldn't stop cheating. She made it clear that her view on cheating was one and done.

Everything she was saying sounded like my relationship with Elle. I admired her for being honest, which made me feel closer to her.

"You don't mind catching the train, do you?" she asked, changing the subject and grabbing a pair of sandals from under the coffee table.

"Not at all," I said.

Chapter Four

Riding the train was something I'd never experienced. I was in awe of the different people and races all gathered, waiting to get off at their destinations. Don't get me wrong, I've ridden public transportation before, but a small bus station is nothing compared to Atlanta's Marta station.

This one woman stood out. She had to be at least six feet tall and look like a model with a smile that would turn heads. She was completely bald, and the way she dressed was unique. She had baggy jogger pants, short black boots, and this weird flower-printed shirt. It could sound better, but it was pure fashion. She was unusual, but it worked for her. Mya grabbed my hand once she saw me staring. I looked at her and smiled. I loved the way her soft hands felt on top of mine.

"Stop staring so hard we're getting off at the next stop," Mya said while grinning.

"I'm sorry, but I love your look, and I couldn't get off this train without telling you that you are beautiful," I said to the mysterious woman, meaning every word. She smiled and said thank you, and she designed everything herself. "No Problem, you look beautiful," I stated as the train stopped.

"She was pretty. I thought you forgot all about me for a second," Mya jokingly said as she stepped on the train. I followed close behind.

"Yeah, she was, and I love her style, but I'm trying to get to know you a little more," I teased and wrapped my arms around her. After riding the escalator to the street, she grabbed my hand, and we walked the two blocks to the park.

"Is this officially a date?" I asked.

"It could be," Mya said.

"Usually, I ask the girl on a date, and it's obvious what I am trying to do. We're walking in the park, holding hands. It seems like a date," I said.

"It could be. If this was a date, I would ask you questions like your past relationships to get to know you better," she said.

"If you want to know anything about me, I don't mind telling you. If this was a date," I said. I pointed to a couple cuddled on a blanket under a tree. "You want to find somewhere to sit?"

"Yes." In front of us was a gazebo with a few people looking out into the lake. "Over there?" Mya pointed.

"Yeah, that's cool. If this were a date, I would tell you that I was married before and was single for a while before I met Elle," I said, reaching the gazebo and taking a seat.

"Married? How long and when?" Mya asked.

"I got married at nineteen to my, I guess you could say, high school sweetheart. The divorce was finalized six months before my graduation. It ended way before that, though," I said.

"So, you've only had two relationships? Your ex-wife and Elle?" Mya asked.

"Technically, one. Elle and I were never together," I said.

"Awe, man," she said.

"Is that bad or something?" I asked with a nervous laugh. My track record was good. I could have bodies lined up, waiting for me to hit them up with that "what's good" text.

"No, it's not bad. It just means you have some deep connections. Trust me, you might feel like you're not in a relationship with Elle, but I am sure she feels differently," she said.

"I don't have any deep connection. I haven't spoken or seen my ex since sitting across from lawyers signing divorce papers. We have zero communication," I said.

"And Elle? Mya asked.

"Yeah. Things haven't been so great lately. Things have run its course. So, what about you? You did say that she was MADLY in love with you," I asked to change the subject of myself.

"It's not a good thing. It's only good if you feel the same way," she said.

"I could use an explanation. You don't feel the same way?" I said.

"Not even close. I've been so busy with school that I didn't see her how she wanted me to. We text and talk on the phone, but I really don't make an effort to try to make anything work. She told me she was in love with me, and I broke it off," she said.

"When did that happen?" I said.

"A few days ago," she said. We both laughed. "I haven't heard from her since."

"Harsh," I said.

"Harsh? I believe in finding your forever person. She wasn't it. Why waste my time or hers?"

Mya said. I didn't know what to say after that statement.

Is that what I was doing to Elle? It's clear that she's not my forever person. Am I wasting her time? What Mya said had me thinking of Elle's and my future. Maybe it was time to let it go, but how do I break up with someone I was never dating?

"Are you ready to keep walking?" I asked.

"Yeah, let's go."

I didn't realize until three hours later that we never let go of each other's hands. It was the perfect day, and for once, I felt content. We ended our walk around the park with her showing me sections of the park she painted from memory in her dorm room. The vibe between us came so effortlessly, and we smiled the entire time. Mya was a breath of fresh air, and I needed to breathe.

"When are you going to show me one of your paintings?" I asked her. Before she could answer, she came to a halt. I felt her body tense up as I glanced to see what had changed her mood. Two females sat on a bench ahead of us. I let go of Mya's hand, confused at what was happening and the sudden change in her energy.

"That's my ex," she said, breaking the awkward silence.

"The "in love one?" I asked, trying to make a joke.

"No. Not that one. Can we go a different way?" Mya asked.

"Yeah, let's walk this way," I said, pointing at the large field's opposite side." It's time to head home anyway. It's getting late." I pulled Mya in the opposite direction. We moved quickly across the grass when one of them called Mya's name. She grabbed my hand tighter and picked up the pace. Eventually, the female caught up to us and grabbed her free arm.

"I know you heard me calling you. What are you doing here, and who the hell is this?" She said and pointed at me. I'm not a fighter. I've had my fair share of brawls, but I wasn't scared of this baby stud. She sized me up and down, but instead of reacting, I smiled and placed my hand on the arch of Mya's back.

"You okay? I asked Mya. Instead of even acknowledging whoever that was. Mya gripped my hand tighter.

"I have nothing to say to you anymore, so excuse me," she told the little girl as we tried to step past her.

"So, that's it? You've been ignoring me for over a year, and now I see you walking in the park hand in hand with her. Then you walk past me like you don't even know me?" she said through clenched teeth, pointing in my direction.

"Don't make a scene. There are a lot of people around, Drea," Mya said as she gripped my hand tighter. I could feel her hand shaking in the palm of mine as we continued to create distance between us and whoever that Drea girl was.

"I'll see you around," she said as her voice trailed in the distance.

The whole ride back to her hotel, Mya was quiet. I watched her stare out the window as we passed through the city. Although her mood changed tremendously, I didn't ask her any questions. I could tell that she was in her head. I sat silently beside her and held her hand as we made our way to the stop.

"What was that about?" I finally asked, walking inside her hotel room.

"I'm sorry, that was the first time I've seen her since our breakup. I'm sorry to put you in that situation," she said, staring out the window. I walked over to her, stood behind her, and wrapped my arms around her.

"I take that it wasn't a pleasant breakup?" I asked.

"Not pleasant at all. More like a restraining order," Mya said, holding onto my arm.

"I like how you acted like I was your girl, though," I joked. "You know I would be whoever you want me to be."

Mya turned around for the first time since the run-in with her ex, Drea, and looked me in the eyes with the same look of pain and hurt I'd seen so many times staring in the mirror.

"Thank you," she said.

"For what? Pretending to be your girl to make your ex jealous?" I said.

"Yes," she laughed. "That and just being there. Thank you for agreeing to go on this date with me."

"So, this is a date?" I said.

She wrapped her hands around my neck and pulled off my hat. We stared at each other. All the pain, uncertainty, heartbreak, and drama of our past didn't matter. We were alone, standing in the window, bodies touching, and emotions high. I closed my eyes and went for her lips. To my surprise, she met me halfway.

Her lips were soft like warm silk as we kissed slowly. At that moment, it was like we understood each other's pain and there was no one in the world but us. I rubbed my hand slowly down the middle of her back, feeling the vibrations of her moans on my lips.

Images of her the first day in those short pajama shorts flashed in my mind as I ran my hand down the arch of her back. Her ass was my goal, and her body was my prize.

IT TOOK A LONG TIME TO GET HERE; IT TOOK A BRAVE GIRL TO TRY….

Alicia Key's single, Brand-New Me, blasted through her iHome speakers. She pulled away quickly. I pulled her back to get her to let the phone ring and stay focused. I did make my goal, and I wanted my prize.

"That's my mom," she whispered, wiggling out of my grip.

"Your mom?" I asked. She nodded. I laughed and let her go. Another day, another time, she will be here for three weeks. I have plenty of time.

"I'll be back," she said, answering the call and walking away. I sat on the couch and grabbed my phone and the remote. I had three new text messages and one missed call.

The missed call was from Toni, but I would call her after I leave. She knew nothing about Mya, and I wanted to keep it that way. Toni could get a little jealous at times. That's just how Toni was; she liked to be the center of attention, and if she weren't, she would find a way to steal the spotlight. Mya told me Toni asked her for her number that day, but Mya gave her the cold shoulder. Toni can't handle rejection, so I could only imagine how she would react if she found out about us.

Elle: Call me when you're on your way, baby.

I miss you, and I'm sorry about earlier.

That's what confuses me about Elle. One minute she's snapping at me for something small, and the next minute, she's being sweet. I could never keep up with her mood swings. Sometimes, it could be something so simple that flips her switch, like me not answering a phone call. Sometimes, she makes me feel like I'm explaining myself like I'm a child.

While Mya talked to her mom in the bedroom, I decided it was time to head out. I had to run home and shower, then head to Elle's. I knew she was pissed at me, but I needed a break from her today. She was becoming too attached, and I felt myself pulling away.

I walked over to the open bedroom door and knocked softly. Mya sat on the edge of the bed with her cell phone to her ear. I whispered to her that I was about to go. She put up a finger to tell me to hold on. I gave her a nod, then pulled out my phone to text Elle. I told her I would be there soon and asked if she wanted anything to eat.

I pressed send and slid my phone back into my pocket. I enjoyed the park, but I was hungry as hell. Shortly after, Mya wrapped up the conversation with her mother.

"I'm sorry about that. My mom doesn't like to get off the phone," she said.

"That's cool. It's getting late anyway. What are you doing tomorrow?" I asked her.

"I'm about to meet my mom for dinner. I might stay the night with her, but I can call you in the morning and let you know if she will keep me busy," she said.

"Okay, cool," I said. I grabbed Mya by the pinky and pulled her close to me. She wrapped her arm around my neck and pulled my forehead to hers. As much as I wanted her, it wasn't the right time. I knew it, and she felt it. I gave her a peck on the forehead and walked out the door.

Chapter Five

After a quick shower back at my apartment, I pulled out a pair of Jordans and grabbed basketball shorts to match and a plain black tee. I wanted to change into something more comfortable. After, I stopped at the package store and bought a bottle of Whiskey.

I used the spare key Elle gave me because of the hours I get home from work at times to enter her apartment. We promise same-day installations for most projects, so sometimes that requires us to work late. So, I would come through the door after eleven p.m., shower quickly, and jump in the bed without her opening an eye. Next, I would wrap my arms around her, pulling her close while I dozed off.

I would wake up to her kissing me goodbye and telling me that she had put something in the oven for me to eat when I woke up. That was our routine most days. We could go days without having an entire conversation. It was like we were stuck in a silent cycle.

The scent of her cooking hit my nose as soon as I walked into her apartment, reminding me that I hadn't eaten anything since earlier that morning. Elle was one hell of a cook because she had to learn to raise her brothers and sisters due to her mom's lack of attention and care. Even though Elle can cook, she doesn't like to anymore, so we order food or go out to eat a lot. Tonight was the first time she had cooked in a while for me, so I knew something was wrong.

"Hey, I'm here," I yelled over her music, locking the door behind me.

"Hey baby, have a seat. I'll be out in a minute," she said. She didn't even look up from stirring whatever was in the pot as I walked past her.

Her studio apartment was huge and always neat, smelling like flowers. The apartment was open, but she used foldable doors to section off the living and bedroom. The Eiffel Tower printed decor added beauty to the studio. Her all-white sofa and loveseat sat in front of the large window overlooking the Atlanta city skyline, with black and white Eifel Tower throw pillows neatly placed in the corners.

I placed the bottle of Whiskey on the coffee table and flipped it to the R&B music channel. I leaned back and laid my head on her couch. Music, to me, was therapeutic, my only escape from the world.

Listening to music, I can block out the world and focus on the song's vibe, beat, lyrics, and emotion. Music tells a story, and sometimes, hearing another person's story is what I need to take my mind off my own. The right song at the right moment could say everything you try to express but can't find the words.

"You must be tired. What did you do today?" Elle said as she walked towards me with two glasses and a can of coke. I smiled. I didn't tell her what kind of alcohol I bought, but she must have known because I love my Whiskey with coke.

"I could have gotten vodka or something," I teased, ignoring her last comment. Walking around the park, all say, hell yeah, I was tired and hungry.

"Every time I ask you to get the alcohol, you come back with the same bottle unless I give you specific instructions," she said. She sat the items down on the coffee table and sat on my lap. Her short pajama shorts exposed her thigh as I rubbed my hand against the softness of her skin. She grabbed my hat, pulled it off my head, and raised my chin. She placed a soft peck on my lips and stared into my face like she was analyzing my thoughts.

After a few seconds, she opened the bottle of Whiskey and poured it into the glasses. Elle popped open the can of coke, filled the cups, and handed one to me. I nervously downed it in one gulp and gave it back to her.

"Thirsty?" she said, stunned by my actions.

"Yeah, a little," I said with a nervous chuckle. I was thrown off. The whole setup felt like a setup. I thought that maybe I should see her take the first bite. Elle hasn't been this sweet in months, and I can't remember the last time she cooked.

Elle refilled my drink and sat it down on the table. She grabbed her glass and took a sip. I'm glad she took a sip first because I could have been poisoned. Elle hasn't really told me about her life, and I've met her friends but no family. She could practice voodoo, and I would have never known.

I grabbed the alcohol out of her hand, turned her around towards me, and kissed her deeply. The timer on the stove began to ring. She quickly jumped up and ran to the kitchen, opening the oven quickly. I laughed and grabbed my drink, sipping this time.

My phone went off, and I knew it was Toni by the ringtone. So, I stepped out on the balcony to take the call. Toni had no filter and had a habit of saying the wrong thing at the wrong time.

"What's up, stalker?" I said after closing the sliding door.

"I've been calling you all day. Where have you been?" Toni responded.

"Dude, it's our first day off in a while. Why are you worried about where I have been? I see you every day," I told her with aggravation. I hate for someone to question me, especially since I was with Elle, and I don't need her wondering about my whereabouts. Elle probably thought I was with her all day.

"Alright, chill. The reason I was stalking you was to see if you wanted to go to this bar with me tonight."

"I can't..."

"I met these two beautiful girls, and they want to meet you," she interrupted.

"Toni!" I yelled.

"Hold on. She's right here. Bro, and she's cute," she said, not letting me get in a word.

"Toni!" I screamed. "I'm with Elle right now. I'm going to hit you up later," I said, not caring if she heard me. I hung up, slipped my phone into my pocket, and returned to the apartment.

I could see Elle sitting on the couch, staring at me through the window. Two plates of food sat on the coffee table. I walked back into the house and admired the chicken, rice, mac and cheese, and string beans sitting on the table. My stomach rumbled with anticipation. I sat beside her, kissed her on her cheek, and grabbed my plate.

"Toni?" Elle asked as I sat down.

"Yeah. She wants to go out tonight, but I'm good," I said, picking up my plate.

Ten minutes later, I was full and on my 3rd cup of Whiskey, feeling the effects of the alcohol and a satisfied belly. Elle grabbed my empty plate and sat it down. I looked over and realized that she had never touched her food. So, I turned my attention to her.

"Are you not hungry?" I asked.

"No. What are we doing, J?" Elle asked, getting straight to the point.

"What do you mean?" I said. I knew what she meant.

"I need an answer today for where this is going. You know I like you, that's no secret, J. You have a key to my apartment despite me having one for yours. I need to know where this is going, and I need to know now," Elle said.

There was so much I wanted to say to her, so much I wish I could say. But that would require me to admit my feelings for Mya. I know I should tell her everything I feel and let her decide where we stand. But how would she handle it?

"I don't know what we're doing," I said, leaning toward her. I hate when a woman says they want to talk and then does nothing but ask you questions.

"Can you at least tell me where your head is? Are we together? Are we friends? Are we dating?" Elle asked.

"This was supposed to be just a chill thing, and feelings got involved. When I met you, I told you I didn't want anything serious, and you understood that. I'm here with you daily because I love being around you, but you always push me to give you more." I wasn't ready to be with Elle in the way she needed me to be. I never lied about any of that. But I wonder if I want to be. "I'm not saying that I don't like you because I do. I wouldn't be here if I didn't," I continued, staring her in the eye.

When I met her, I was only separated for a short while and had just moved to Atlanta. She hit me up online to show me around the city, and things took off afterward. We never spoke of a relationship. She just started acting like we were in one. Maybe I was wrong for never correcting her and giving her time like we were together, but I never wanted things to get serious. I got used to it and let it happen. She was that friend I could talk to about anything; eventually, her feelings got involved.

"I've been here for six months, stuck by your side from day one, holding you when you needed to be held, comforting you when you asked for comfort, and what am I getting in return? I'm here every day and every night at your disposal, playing wife only to get pushed back into friendship status. You're sitting here saying you don't want a relationship, but you took the key to my apartment. You're the one who comes here every night after work and curls up in this bed with me. I didn't push none of this on you, and I'm damn sure not pressuring you," she screamed.

I downed the rest of my drink as if it were the cure to the rising pressure in my chest. After, I poured another.

"I didn't come over here to argue with you. You said you wanted to talk, well talk! Stop raising your voice like you're crazy," I said.

"If a relationship isn't what you want, I can't continue waiting and hoping you change your mind. I'm not asking for your hand in marriage, but you're sitting here treating me like I'm stressing you," Elle stated calmly.

"What do you want from me, Elle?" I asked. I was defeated and wanted this conversation to be over so I could enjoy this alcohol running through my blood and keep my high from today's events. I started to wonder what Mya was doing at that moment. Was she enjoying dinner with her mom? Was she thinking about me?

"I don't want anything from you that you don't want to give willingly. All I'm saying is my feelings are getting involved, and since you don't want a relationship, I need to protect myself, and playing house with a person who doesn't want to commit is not helping. I need space!"

She was right. We were acting like we were together. In a way, I wanted a relationship without the title. While recovering from my divorce, I needed someone to be there for me physically and emotionally. I wasn't thinking about Elle's feelings because giving someone so much of your time and energy, sooner or later, it's only human for them to want more. I wish it were later, but I couldn't control another woman's feelings.

We sat in silence after that, trying to figure out the right words to say. I wanted to push Elle onto the couch, tickle her until she cried, and then plant kisses on her face and neck to make it better. I wanted her to playfully knee me in my stomach and push me off her, then climb on top of me to pin me down to get me back. I wanted to run around the house playing and laughing as we used to when we first met. But instead, we sat there looking at each other, waiting for someone to say something. But nothing came out.

"Finish your drink, and you can leave," she said, turning her attention to the television.

I did just that. I was mentally exhausted from the fight and physically exhausted from the stroll through the park with Mya. I needed some sleep, and it was clear that I wouldn't get any at Elle's that night. I guess we had officially broken up. Maybe it was the alcohol, but I wasn't even sad. Maybe a little drunk as I danced my way to my car. I felt relieved, and like I said, she wasn't my forever girl, so why waste her time?

After stumbling to my truck, I realized I might have had more to drink than I thought. There was no way that I was driving. It was one o'clock in the morning, and I could barely put the key into the ignition.

I called an Uber, and because Elle lived in the middle of downtown Atlanta, it was only a seven-minute wait. I wanted to text Mya so badly, but with the alcohol in my system and my emotions on high, I knew that was a horrible idea. Instead, I stood waiting for an Uber, replaying the argument between Elle and me.

Chapter Six

I woke up the following day, passed out on my loveseat, fully dressed, with a dead phone on my chest. I picked it up and plugged it into the charger I kept on the side of the sofa. As soon as the phone powered on, I unlocked it quickly and went to my messages. I clicked on Mya's text thread—no new messages.

I put my phone on the coffee table and walked to my room. I hopped in the shower, brushed my teeth, and prepared for my lazy day. I was supposed to spend the weekend with Elle, but we decided to give each other space last night. I plan to catch up on some episodes of my favorite TV shows and enjoy the day alone.

I hopped on the couch, grabbed the remote, and strolled through Netflix. After finding a movie, I got comfortable and grabbed my phone.

INTELLEGENT_ELLE:

Step one, healing.

INTELLEGENT_ELLE:

Step two is acceptance.

INTELLEGENT_ELLE:

Step three, move one.

Elle's tweets had me in my feelings. Losing Elle wasn't easy. She is a great woman, but Elle is now looking for a wife. She is ready to plan a wedding and have babies, but I have just begun making real money. I love my apartment, building a nice savings, and just got divorced. I'm twenty-four, and she's thirty-seven. I still have a life to live. I wasn't ready for what she asked me for, so I had to let her go. A call from Mya knocked me out of my thoughts.

"Hey, what are you doing right now?" Mya asked.

"Nothing at all. I was going to find something to watch and be lazy all day," I said.

After giving her my address, she insisted that she pick it up on her way over to save me a trip. Twenty minutes later, Mya stood at my door holding a food bag.

"Why didn't you call me when you were downstairs? I could have helped. Did you have problems parking or getting inside?" I asked, grabbing the bag.

"No, you must have told the stewardess that I was coming because they led me straight up," she said.

"Yeah, I did, and good," I said. I walked her into the living room. We both sat on the sofa as I dug through the food bag.

"You have a nice place. I like that you don't live in a high-rise apartment complex," Mya said as she scanned the room. "This place reminds me of a New York flat because of the exposed pipelines in the ceiling." I handed Mya a plate of pancakes, sausage, and eggs.

"That's why I fell in love with this place," I said, taking a bite of sausage. "I wanted to be in the heart of downtown, but I didn't want to live in a crowded high rise. This building only has thirty flats, as they call it, and six floors. The private parking is what sold me as well.

"Wait, you watch Stranger Things?" Mya asked, noticing my "continue watching" tab on Netflix.

"I'm so far behind. I can never find the time to watch tv." I spent all my time off with Elle, and Stranger Things is not the kind of show she enjoys. Elle preferred crime shows and documentaries. I hated them, so we usually settled on movies. “I decided today

I could spend it catching up. Wait, assuming you watch Stanger Things as well?" I asked.

"I love it. I'm all caught up and waiting on the next season, " Mya admitted. We smiled, realizing that we had another thing in common. I pressed play to break the silence and tension in the room. After finishing the rest of our breakfast, I pulled Mya close to me, cradling her like a kid with their favorite bear. She relaxed in my chest and placed a soft kiss on my chin.

"I want to apologize about yesterday," she whispered, rubbing her fingers up and down my forearm.

"You have nothing to apologize for. If only you knew how my night went," I said.

"I take it that you finished that argument," Mya said.

"How did you know?" I laughed. "Something you said really sat with me."

"Yeah, what's that?"

"About not wasting time if they aren't your person," I said.

Her phone began to vibrate in her pocket. She quickly hopped up and answered in a hurry.

"Hey, Mom," Mya said as she reached for her car keys and bag. "Yeah, I'm not too far away. I'll meet you there in ten." Mya grabbed my hand as she led us to the front door. "Love you too."

"You got to run so soon?" I asked as she ended the call. I couldn't help but notice how soft her hands were.

"I'm sorry. I promised that I would spend the day shopping with her. I wanted to see you, but I have to meet her in a few. Can I call you later?" she said apologetically.

"In that case, I'm happy that I could enjoy breakfast with you," I said, trying not to sound clingy. The truth? I would have loved to spend the day cuddling her on the couch, kissing her soft-looking lips, and rubbing her silky thighs.

"Thank you for that, by the way." she said. We stopped at the door, and Mya turned to face me. I pulled her close and smiled. She smiled back. "I have to go," she whispered and bit her lip.

"Call or text me. I'll be here," I stated honestly. Mya gave me a peck on the cheek and disappeared down the hallway. I locked the door and hopped back on the sofa, pressing play on the TV. After watching a few episodes, I fell asleep until I received a text from Mya, knocking me out of my slumber. She asked if she could Facetime me later. I wrote her back and told her it was fine.

The rest of the day was spent lying on the couch, eating potato chips, and watching TV. When I decided to unstick myself from the sofa, Elle still hadn't contacted me. That wasn't like her. No matter how upset she became, she would always text me to try to make up. I guess she was over me this time. I didn't know whether to be bitter or content with her decision. After all, it was what I wanted. Or was it?

After drying off, I retrieved my phone from the coffee stand and checked my messages. Disappointed that the notification bar was empty, loneliness began to take over. I walked to the kitchen, grabbed a glass and a bottle of whiskey, and poured myself a drink. I downed the first glass, then another, feeling the effects of the whiskey take over my body. Afterward, I grabbed a water bottle and walked back into the room. It was after ten o'clock, and I was ready to call it a night. Just as I was lying down, my phone rang. It was Mya.

"Hey, you!" she said through the camera.

"Hey, how was your day?"

"It was nice. I didn't realize how much I missed my mom. She told me she has a boyfriend," she said.

"A boyfriend," I said.

"Yes, a boyfriend."

"How do you feel about that?" I said.

"I don't know. My mom hasn't dated anyone since my dad passed, but I mean, it was over five years ago. She deserves to be happy. Everyone does," she said.

"I'm happy you're happy that she's happy," I said. We both laughed.

"I wanted to also apologize for yesterday. I am so embarrassed."

"Don't be embarrassed. I think you handled yourself well," I said.

"I think this is the first time we ever sat on camera," she said.

"Is it? We should do this more often. I enjoy seeing your face," I said.

"Hopefully, you can see my face in person soon. Do you have to work tomorrow?" Mya asked.

"Yeah. I don't know what time I'll be home. I can call you when I make it. What are you doing tonight?" I said.

"Movie night with my mom. She's in the shower right now. I'm waiting until she comes back downstairs," she said.

"Oh, what are you watching?" I asked.

"Her and my dad's favorite movie, Brown Sugar," she said.

"I love that movie. It's a classic for sure," I said.

"It's the love story for me. Sometimes you can search your whole life for someone who has been in front of you," she said.

"Is that right?" I asked.

"Yeah, it is. Get some rest. I just wanted to see your face before I called it a night," she admitted.

"Thank you for calling," I said.

"Call me tomorrow after work?" Mya asked.

"Yes, ma'am. Enjoy your movie night," I said.

"Sweet dreams!"

After hanging up, it didn't take long for me to fall asleep. We had a job two hours from the city that next day installing new countertops, and I wanted to get a fresh start in hopes of beating Atlanta morning traffic.

Chapter Seven

The following day, I sat in the passenger seat with Toni. We were headed to yet another job, and I could get there fast enough. Toni was in the middle of telling me what happened the night before with her dates. I half-listened, my mind on a text I received from Mya.

Mya: I keep apologizing for the park situation, but the more I think about it, the more I feel embarrassed.

I felt weird having to hide Mya from Toni. Of course, we always confided in each other, but something told me this was something I should keep to myself for a while. I wanted to tell her everything. I needed someone to talk to. Mya wasn't a secret, but Toni has always been Team Elle. She loves to make jokes about her being my next wife.

"Are you there? Did you hear what I said?" Toni asked, interrupting my thoughts.

"I heard you. I'm listening. When are you meeting up with them again?" I said to her, trying to distract her and keep her talking. I texted Mya back and told her I had forgotten about the park, but that was a lie. But when she told me that she hadn't been honest with me about the situation, I couldn't stop thinking about what that could be.

"I can have them come to my apartment when we get off," she said.

"I don't know, man. Elle asked me to chill with her." I lied, but I needed to hear what Mya had to say. What could she have lied about, and why did she need to lie when we've been open and honest with each other? We decided to meet later to discuss it, and the day couldn't move quicker.

"Bro, you're always with Elle. I thought you were single?" Toni said.

"I am. But you want me to come over there to try and get some ass, and I already got some at home," I laughed, playing off my feelings for Mya. To be honest, Elle and I haven't had sex in so long; we probably forgot how.

When Elle and I first met, we couldn't keep our hands off each other. We probably had sex every day for the first month and a half. We couldn't keep our hands off each other, and things slowed. I've tried multiple times, even having her get all dolled up and taking her to upscale restaurants. We would flirt and touch each other under the table as the expensive wine flowed through our bloodstreams to get back to her place and pass out immediately. It had been months since we touched each other.

"Okay, you got a point. But the offer is still open if you change your mind," Toni said.

"Cool," I said, remembering when I first met Toni. Toni and I were not destined to be friends because we were from two totally different worlds, but we managed to click immediately, and though we may have fallen out a few times in college, we always made up and got back cool.

I was sitting in the lobby of our dorm, letting this cute girl braid my hair. A couple of her friends were in the corner playing cards and talking shit about her braiding my hair for free. But I knew she had a crush on me. Of course, she wasn't gay, just gay for me.

I was never the one for big crowds and didn't have a lot of friends, but I was a ladies' boi, so all my friends were fems or straight women. I never got along with other studs and only ran with a few males I thought were cool.

One of her friends started debating about light-skinned men versus dark-skinned men. Toni, also known as the dorm's clown, walked into the conversation with her entourage of studs who lived in the door behind her. Toni chimed in to add her love for dark-skin women.

"Yo, light-skinned, what do you think?" Toni asked me. Of course, I wasn't even looking their way, but she knew I heard their conversation since they were so loud.

"Aint nothing sexier than a pretty dark-skinned girl. They may be hard to find, but when you see them, you can't deny their beauty," I said. Toni got up and walked towards me. My friend was on my last braid, which I was happy with cause the shit hurt like hell.

"Yo, what's up? My name is Toni," she said, dapping me up.

"J," was all I said in return.

"Yall niggas lame! Yall going to run after the same redbone, but that's cool. That leaves all the sexy dark ones for us," she said, hitting me on my shoulder. From that day on, we were tight like glue.

Toni was from Tallahassee and a true Floridan from the accent and locs down to the gold grill and Florida tattoo on her neck. She made college fun, and in return, I kept her focused on the books.

We both majored in construction with a minor in business management. We both wanted to build. It didn't matter what it was; we loved using our hands.

Throughout the rest of our college years, we always had the same classes. At times, we rotated on who went to class that week, although it was mostly me because Toni would often be so messed up after a night of partying in the city that when it was her turn to attend class, I had to go to her dorm, wake her up, and push her to head to class. After a while, I just said forget it and went anyway.

We pushed each other for four years. I should say that I pushed her for four years and, after graduation, began building our successful company.

We pulled up to the customer's home and began unpacking our tools. If we didn't encounter significant problems, we could complete everything in one day. That was the goal.

The entire day, I was quiet. My mind was stuck on Mya and what it was that she couldn't tell me. I couldn't even focus, causing me to hit my finger a few times with the hammer.

"What are you trying to do? Take your hand off?" Toni asked as I held my thumb in my hand, trying to ease the pain.

"My finger slipped," I said.

"Go whip down the countertops so we can wrap this up before you hurt yourself. We don't have company insurance," Toni said.

It was after five o'clock when we were finally finished. Mya had texted me earlier that day to say she wouldn't be able to hang with me and would call me tomorrow. I was slightly upset because I had been waiting to hear what she had to tell me, but I told her that was fine. I knew she was coming to spend time with her mom during her break. Because Mya would be busy, I decided to take Toni's offer and chill with her and her friends. The last thing I wanted to do was be at home in my feelings. I might have messed around and tried fixing things with Elle, but I knew I needed to let her go. I didn't want to keep leading her on.

We dropped the work truck off at the storage, and Toni followed me to my apartment. Traffic in downtown Atlanta was always worse in the afternoon, so Toni decided to chill at my place since the garage was close to my apartment until it died down, and then we would drive to her place.

Toni sat down on my couch while I went to my room and dressed. Toni didn't like it in the downtown area. She would say it's too many white people. From what she told me, Toni grew up in the hood and will die in the hood. I believed her because we made six figures a year, and she moved to a $600 two-bedroom apartment on Memorial Drive. A swap meet mall, a few fast-food restaurants, and a used car dealership were down the street from her apartment.

My apartment was much smaller than hers, and I was paying almost $2000 a month, but I was in the middle of downtown. Connected to my building was a coffee shop, a bar, and a small gym. Depending on what I needed, everything could be within walking distance. I loved city life and especially enjoyed living in the heart of Atlanta.

Toni was the opposite of me in so many ways. She enjoyed being out in Decatur, and I dreaded every time I had to hop on Highway 285. I even hated going to Toni's apartment because it was always somebody sitting on the step smoking weed, Newport's, or a black-n-mild. I'm a country girl. I grew up in the suburbs of a small town surrounded by people I've known my whole life.

Toni grew up differently than me. While I was raised in a Christian, two-parent household, Toni was raised by her mom. Her father was doing life in prison and had been since she was five, and her brother was ten. Toni loved and worshiped him just like the people in her neighborhood, with nothing but respect. Toni's brother took over the family business and earned his street credit before he turned eighteen.

Toni's brother ensured his little sister needed nothing when she was away for college, with her being the only freshman riding in a fresh-off-the-lot Chevy Cruise. I also had a car my freshman year, but it was my dad's old pickup truck that I had been driving since I was fourteen. My parents got a fresh coat of paint and new tires for my graduation present and got the inside detailed. To me, it was brand new.

Toni also loved her females with a little hood in them. I prefer city girls, preferably one with a high-paying job and a decent vocabulary. She would call the women she dated "young and dumb" and prides herself on controlling them using money and gifts. Toni feeds off females that need her. As I said, we were complete opposites.

"All these damn channels you are paying for and ain't shit on?" Toni said from my couch. I was in my room trying to find something to wear.

"Don't worry about what I do with my money. At least I'm spending it on quick weaves and blunts for them ghetto females you mess with," I said from my closet.

"Fuck you! It's cheaper than dropping stacks on those hoes to get a piece of mediocre ass. You break more bread than me on these females, taking them to expensive ass restaurants and shit," she said while laughing.

"Yeah, but the pussy is good and tight, not used and abused like them hood rats you like," I said while laughing.

"Don't knock it until you try it. Just hurry your cute ass up, ole ironing ya draws type nigga," she said. We both laughed at that comment.

I pulled out some black jeans, a burgundy and gray button-down shirt, my black vest, and my black and gray Jordans. I grabbed my burgundy and black Jordan fitted to top it off. I placed my outfit on my bed the way that I would put it on. I took a step back and admired the fit. I was a pretty boi, and Toni loved picking on me. I take pride in my appearance.

"Hurry up, cute ass nigga," Toni yelled from the living room.

"I'm coming," I said.

After about an hour, we were out the door. Toni hopped in her car, and I jumped in my truck. We headed towards Highway 285. Traffic had eased up a bit, so it was a smooth ride to Toni's apartment. During the drive there, all I could think about was Elle.

How could she blow me off like that? A few days ago, things were fine, and we were happy. Or so I thought. I understand where she came from, but we had a good thing going. The more I thought about Elle, the madder I got, knowing that she knew the situation beforehand, and if she couldn't handle it, I could have found someone who could.

How could she be upset with a situation she agreed to? Things were fine a few months ago. I was still trying to figure out what had changed. Females always want more. Although Elle was avoiding me, the conversation wasn't over. I was going to talk to Elle, eventually.

As much as I knew she wasn't my person, I didn't want things to end that way. I loved and respected Elle and was thankful she came into my life when she did. I just wanted her to know that and not end on bad terms. I think!

Lost in my thoughts, it felt like I was driving for ten minutes, but I was pulling into Toni's complex thirty minutes later. I parked my car next to hers and got out. We walked up to the second floor. She opened her door, and I went straight to the game room.

Toni's apartment was a lot bigger and cheaper than mine. She had a two-bedroom; she made the other room into a workout/game room. Toni was a huge video gamer; I was too, but not as big as her. Her living room wasn't as decorated as her game room, with only one couch and a coffee table. She never used the living room because she lived in her game room.

Her game room was bigger than the size of my bedroom. It had a small futon sofa resting against the back wall and two adult-size bean bags everyone loved.

A rack of free weights and a treadmill were on the wall next to the bags. The entertainment center held a 55-inch 3D TV, which was Toni's prized possession. A bunch of PS4 games, a console, and a small collection of movies. On the opposite wall of the free weights was a small refrigerator that she kept filled with bottled water and Gatorade.

I sat on one of the bean bags and grabbed the remote and PS4 controller. I popped in Call of Duty and began to play while she got ready. The girls were supposed to arrive in an hour.

Twenty minutes later, Toni came wearing army-printed shorts, a lime green and black shirt that read: I Only Love Money, and some fresh green and black Nike's. Her shoulder-length dreads were pulled back in a loose ponytail, and a black fitted to the back. I laughed at her shirt and handed her the controller.

"Yo, have you talked to Elle?" Toni asked, looking at the TV.

"No, not today. I thought I would have got a text by now, but I didn't," I said.

"She's probably waiting to see if you would hit her up first," she responded. We started Multiplayer and played a few rounds.

"Yeah, you are probably right. I'm not going to call first, though. If I do, Elle might think that I want to make it official, and I don't," I said, finally admitting it to myself.

"Oh, she's asking for a relationship now?" Toni asked.

"I guess so. I'm not trying to do all of that," I said.

"I feel you. You just divorced that crazy-ass wife of yours. I would need about a five-year break from relationships," she said. We both laughed.

"Tell me about it," I said. Toni had a point. I spent the last seven years with my wife and the only person I ever slept with. Well, besides Elle. All I knew was that I didn't want to spend another seven years with someone I wasn't happy with.

"You know Elle is a real woman? Why won't ya'll just get married already? You love her, and she damn sure loves your ass," Toni said.

"I do not love Elle. I don't even know if I like her. She's crazy jealous," I said.

"Duh! That's why she doesn't like me. I know she thinks I have you around other women and shit," she said. Before I could answer the question, there was a knock on the door.

While Toni answered the door, I went to the bathroom. When I came out, I could hear them talking in the kitchen. I entered the kitchen. Toni was in the middle of pouring four shots of Captain Morgan.

However, I needed a double shot when I saw the two girls. One of the girls, whom Toni was rubbing all on, had a quick weave that looked as thick as a helmet. When she smiled, this girl had the nerve to have one gold tooth in her mouth.

She was slim and thick, though, with some little shorts that barely covered her ass, a yellow Aeropostale shirt, and all-white Air Force Ones. She had a big booty to be so petite; I figured that caught Toni's attention. A tiny waist and a fat ass always made her crazy.

"How are you doing? I'm Chelsea," the other girl said. I looked over at her, forgetting that she was in the kitchen. Chelsea looked a little better. She had long, natural hair that stopped just past her shoulders. Chelsea wasn't as small as her friend but wasn't big. She was curvy. I never got the first girl's name because as soon as I walked in, she and Toni disappeared into the back room. I was left to entertain Chelsea.

"J," was all I said as I walked over, took my shot, poured another, and downed that one. Tonight was going to be a long night, I thought to myself.

Chelsea wore skinny beige jeans, a red and white shirt cut low enough to show her cleavage and sandals. She seemed quiet and more laid back than the other one. I made another drink and her one and walked to the game room.

"You want to watch a movie? I'm not sure how long they will be or even if they are coming back out tonight," I said.

"No, but we can hope on Call of Duty zombies," she said while grabbing the remote.

"You game?" I asked her while smiling. I never met a female gamer. Elle had a Wii but only used it for dancing games and working out.

"Yep, and you better keep up. If I have to keep reviving you, I'm kicking you off," she said.

"Deal! You talk a lot of games. How about we make it a little more interesting? If you go down, you take a shot," I said.

"Ok, bet," she said while leaving the room. Ten seconds later, she returned with a bottle of peach Cîroc. "If we are playing like that, we're taking shots of this, yawl not about to have me on my ass drunk off some Captain Morgan." She handed me the bottle.

About an hour and five shots later, we were tipsy and enjoying each other's company. We learned a lot about each other. I found out that the other girl was her cousin, and her name was Shondra. They were both from Columbus, GA, but Shondra had been in Atlanta for five years. Chelsea moved here to get away from her abusive ex-girlfriend, and she's been living with her cousin till she got back on her feet. She worked at a salon in the area doing hair and eventually wanted to open her own. She clarified that she was not responsible for her cousin's hair.

"Be careful about the studs you run into in Atlanta because these females here are a trip," I warned her, still focusing on the game.

"Trust me, I don't have time for a relationship. Hell, I'm sleeping on a sofa. I need to get myself together first," Chelsea said.

"I feel you on that," I said.

Toni and Shondra finally decided to join the party. It was obvious they had just finished having sex because Shondra's quick weave needed extra glue and a brush, and Toni's dreads were hanging instead of in the ponytail. Chelsea and I looked at each other and burst out laughing.

"Glad you decided to join us," I said.

"What yawl doing in here?" she said and flopped on the floor.

We had already cut the game off and decided to watch Kevin Hart stand up. Toni and Shonda sat behind us, kissing and touching each other like they didn't just come from having sex. It started to get a little uncomfortable for Chelsea and me, so we decided to sit on the balcony.

"They're probably going to fuck again," Chelsea said while lighting a cigarette.

"Yeah," I said, sitting down and taking out my phone. Elle crossed my mind, and I wanted to go on her Twitter to see what she was doing.

INTELLEGENT_ELLE

I want to call her so bad to see

what she is doing, but I'm done waiting on her.

INTELLEGENT_ELLE

Ugh this is so hard! We never went

this long without talking.

INTELLEGENT_ELLE

Am I stupid for loving someone

who's not ready to be loved?

INTELLEGENT_ELLE

I told her how I feel she doesn't care.

I was so into Elle's Twitter page that I didn't hear Toni and Shondra.

"Yo, what's wrong, bruh? Why are you sitting there looking like somebody stole your puppy? Is that Elle? She wants you home already?" Toni said.

Elle had to come better than that to get me to leave. No, I didn't want a relationship and had my reasons. I also knew I didn't want to live like Toni. I don't like to be in the streets. The alcohol had my feelings all jacked up. Part of me wanted to run to Elle, and the other half wanted to pursue these feelings for Mya. I don't know if it was the alcohol talking or how I truly felt. At that moment, I was ready to hop on the highway, knock on Elle's door, and make love until she forgot about this little space, she wanted between us. Maybe then things would become apparent.

"YO, EARTH TO J!" Toni said, waving her hand before me. I was so spaced out thinking about this girl that I forgot that a mini party was happening. Toni had turned on the surround sound in the game room and was blasting Wale while she rolled up. Usually, I don't smoke, but I joined in on the rotation. I needed to get my mind off Elle.

"Bruh, what's on your mind? What's going on?" Toni asked, passing me the blunt.

"I'll tell you later," I said. I took a puff.

After the blunt had gone around rotation a couple more times, I was high as hell. Higher than I had ever been, and I couldn't get Elle out of my mind. No matter how many shots I took or the times I hit the blunt, she consumed my every thought. The more I thought about her, the more I felt like she was giving me an alternative: all of her or none of her. I felt my back against the wall. I don't know if it was the weed or the alcohol, but my feelings went through the roof, and my emotions skyrocketed.

"Man, females are crazy," I said out loud to no person.

"What did Elle do to you this time?" Toni said.

I was starting to feel more relaxed and, with the influence, slightly more talkative. "Elle is pushing my back against the wall, giving me the alternative to either get serious with her or she's going to walk. Damn, man, why can't shit stay the same? I'm not messing with anybody else, I'm always with her ass, and I give her any and everything she wants. She is pushing me too far, too fast." I said, finally getting everything off my chest.

"Damn, yawl aren't messing around no more? When did this happen?" Toni said while lighting up another blunt.

"Last night, we got into this big argument, telling me to be with her or she can't do this anymore. I haven't talked to her since I stormed out of her apartment," I said, grabbing the blunt from Toni and taking a pull.

"That's fucked up. She knew that you just ended a seven-year relationship and shit. I wouldn't be ready to jump into anything serious, either. It wasn't even a year ago. Yeah, she is tripping, man," Toni said. I felt better that someone understood my point of view.

"What did you tell her?" Chelsea asked me.

"I told her I wasn't ready, and it was just too much pressure," I said.

"It just sounds like you want to go out and do your own thing and keep her along for the ride. Maybe she needs to feel special. What exactly are you not ready for? Committing?" Chelsea asked.

"I'm already committed to her. I haven't slept with anyone since I met her." I said.

"So why is it so hard to give her the title if you're already committed to her," she asked. Mya popped into my head.

"Because "titles" complicate things. I love doing what I do for Elle, spending time with her, but it's not an obligation. I do it because I enjoy her company, and like you said, if I'm already committed to her, why is a title so important? Why would you put that much pressure on someone knowing how they feel about the situation and knowing there's a chance they might leave? That's only complicating a perfect situation because you get too involved with your feelings. I don't understand you, fems. You want what I'm giving you, but with a title, and you would jeopardize everything instead of enjoying the moment and letting things play out on their own." I said, getting irritated.

Even before Mya came into the picture, Elle had distanced herself from me, questioning our relationship and starting arguments about simple things. The pressure was there before I ever met Mya.

"Damn right," Toni jumped in.

"I'm just saying maybe all she wants is a little reassurance," Chelsea said.

There was a brief silence. I didn't want to continue the conversation; I was starting to get aggravated. It didn't make sense to me, but I knew I needed to talk to Elle sooner or later.

"Spades, anyone?" Toni said, breaking the silence.

The night ended with all of us sitting in Toni's game room, playing spades, talking, and listening to music. I was ready to leave once my high went down and my buzz started to subside. I looked at my phone; it was after 1 o'clock in the morning.

"Yo, I'm about to head home," I told Toni while getting up and putting on my jacket.

"Alright, cool, I'm getting tired, my damn self," she said.

Chelsea and I exchanged numbers, and I said my goodbyes to her and her cousin. Then, I grabbed my keys and headed to the door while Toni followed me.

"J, about you and Elle, you need to go talk to her. I talk a lot of shit about females, but you and Elle are good together. She can't just throw you to the wolves like that; there must be more to the situation. That girl loves you, and I don't think she would jeopardize your relationship like that. But first, you need to think about what you want. Talk to her." She said as we walked out the door.

"She doesn't listen, man. I tried. She wants a relationship, and I don't. I'm not about to go over there with the same argument to leave the same way. I love her. I do, man, you know that, but not like that. Damn, I was locked down for seven years, and it feels good to breathe. Can I enjoy the moments?" I said, standing outside my car door.

"I don't blame you. Elle might can't stand me, but she is a good woman. You have some decisions to make, bruh. It would help if you talked to her," Toni said.

After that, we gave each other a half hug. I hopped in my car and headed to the highway. Once I made it on the freeway, I couldn't help but think about what Chelsea said. She may need some assurance.

It was two a.m., and I was tipsy, but I had to see and talk to her. We needed to get this straight. If a title was all she wanted, it was worth a try. What about Mya, though? She had a girl back in Florida. She lived so far away, and what about the whole park situation? I tried to convince myself that Mya was bad for me, even though I couldn't deny spark and connection. Elle deserved more, and I had made up my mind that I was going to work things out with her.

I needed to figure out a way to make it up to Elle. I hopped on the highway and headed straight to Elle's. After parking, I hopped out, let the cool air sober me up, and went to her door.

Chapter Eight

"Who is it?" Elle screamed from inside her apartment. I was at her door at two a.m., banging on it like I was the cops. I didn't want to call her out of fear that she might tell me not to come over. I needed to see her, talk to her, and hold her. Shit, I was happy that she was there.

"It's me," I said.

She opened the door with a robe wrapped around her waist. She looked at me, and I could still see the hurt in her eyes. We stood there, looking at each other as if time stood still. The silence was so thick and sharp that it cut through the air rapidly.

I didn't know what to say. Standing there felt so unreal, and even though it was only last night that we had our fight, it felt like years. Don't get me wrong. We've had arguments before, but this one felt different.

"What are you doing here?" she asked.

"I need to talk to you. Elle, I'm sorry I stormed out. I just felt pressured, and I didn't like the feeling. "I said. Maybe it's the alcohol, but I just wanted to climb in the bed, wrap my arms around Elle, and pass out like we've done so many times before.

Elle stepped out into the hallway and closed the door.

"Damn I can't come in, that's what we do now?" I said.

"You said you need to talk, so talk," she said, folding her arms.

"Who is in there," I asked, moving her to the side and attempting to enter the apartment. I've known this girl for six months, and not once, no matter what we argue about, have I ever had to carry on a conversation outside her door. "Elle, who is in there?' I asked her again. Apparently, she didn't hear me the first time.

"Since you want to talk about what I'm doing, let's talk about what you've been doing. I know you were at the park with some girl yesterday. You were holding hands and shit. Then you come here talking about you're only fucking with me. No wonder why you want to stay single. You know why you can't come into my apartment, J? Because you lied about everything, I thought we had. Which isn't shit. Even without the title J, that's fucked up. I know we're not together, but you have told me plenty of times that you're only messing with me. You led me on this entire time," she said, damn near in tears.

"I'm not sleeping with that girl." We haven't had sex. I wasn't lying. There was a brief silence, long enough for me to hear someone cough through her door. "Elle, who is that?" I asked her.

"I have to go. I'm sure you have somewhere else to be tonight," Elle said, walking into her apartment. I put my hand on the door to push it open, but my pride stopped me.

"Enjoy yourself," I said instead. I must be crazy. Fuck Elle. It's funny how the universe works. I came here to make up with her but look at that! If I had any doubts about where we stood before, I was 100% sure it was over now. There was no way I was going to be with Elle after that. So yeah, we were done. I was done. Elle was a distant memory. I had made up my mind.

I sat in my car, picked up my phone, and dialed Mya's number. I never texted her earlier, so she might want to hear from me. On the 4th ring, she picked up, sounding half asleep and sexy as hell.

"Hello," she said.

"Hey, it's J. I know you're sleeping, but I wanted to hear your voice," I could hear her smile, so I continued. "I got your text, but I'm not going to lie. I hoped you would change your mind if I gave you time to think."

"Why are you up? What time is it? Where are you?" she said, still trying to wake up.

"I just pulled up to my apartment from Toni's, and I had to call you. I've been thinking about your text all day," I said. It wasn't the whole truth, but it was close enough. I was hoping she would ask me to come over. I didn't want to sleep alone. Even if we just lay there, I was cool with that.

"Are you drunk?" She asked.

"A little, but I'm sure I can make it to your spot," I said.

"Are you trying to get in my bed, J? I'm not sure that's a good idea," she said. I could hear her moving around.

"We don't have to have sex. I just want to lay with you, clothes on. I promise," I said.

"You sure you can drive? I can come to you," she said.

"I would never let a lady leave her bed at this hour. I will be there in ten minutes," I said. She giggled and told me she would tell the front desk to send me right up.

I hung up the phone and put my truck in reverse. Fuck Elle! How is she going to have another female up in there? That's some dirty-ass shit, and the main reason I don't want her ass. My mother always told me never to trust them as far as you can throw them. I guess she was right.

No longer was I feeling drunk or high. I was pissed! Pissed at Elle for pulling some shit like that. I needed to get my head straight before I saw Mya. Before getting out of the truck, I went to Elle's Twitter page to see what she wrote:

INTELLEGENT_ELLE

Far from stupid... good night

I went to Mya's room and knocked on the door. She opened the door, looking exotic as hell. Her black boy shorts hugged her ass perfectly. The lace material on the bottom of the boy shorts gave me a sneak peek of her perfectly round ass. I wanted to grip them right there. Hold them in the palm of my hand.

Mya had her hair to one side of her head, hanging just above her breast. Her eyes were puffy, and she still had lines from the pillow on the side of her face. Still, she smiled, and it felt good to feel wanted.

I stepped in without saying a word, took off my shirt, and threw it on the sofa. That argument with Elle had me hot, but Mya's presence seemed to cool me down.

"You are just making yourself at home, huh?" Mya said.

"I'm sorry, I'll get it," I said, wrapping my hands around her.

"Hey," she said and wrapped her arms around my neck.

She felt so good and soft. Everything with Elle went out of my head. All my problems and all my pain didn't seem to matter anymore. Somehow, she drained me of my worries, and I knew I could hold her forever if it felt this good. She let out a sigh and hugged me tighter.

"What's wrong?" I asked, removing her arms around my neck to see her face.

"I'm scared about how you feel about the park situation. That was out of my element. So, I hope you don't have any negative thoughts of me," she said. How could I think negatively of her when I was banging on someone's door ten minutes ago, begging them to talk to me?

"If anything has changed, I want to get to know you more than ever," I told her. She took my hand and led me to the bedroom. I sat on her bed, taking off my shoes. She sat on a chair, watching me. "You look sexy even when you wake up."

"Thank you, and you look sexy every time I see you. I hope you are not planning on getting any. I don't sleep on second dates," she said.

"Oh, I made it to the second date, huh?" I said. I folded my jeans and sat them on my shoes in the corner.

"It's definitely not a booty call," she said.

"So, what do I get on a second date?" I said and pulled her up from the chair and onto my lap. I wrapped her legs around my waist and kissed her softly. She removed my hat, undid my ponytail, and rubbed her fingers through my hair. I moaned and sucked her neck. I felt her legs grip my waist tighter as she arched her back and gripped the back of my neck with both hands. I leaned her over the bed and climbed between her legs. Suddenly, she put her hand on my stomach and pushed me away.

"What's wrong?" I asked her.

"No sex, remember," Mya said.

I kissed her softly on her lips, then her cute dimple, and lastly, her neck. I slid from between her legs and laid down in front of her. We both got under the cover. She moved closer and threw her leg over my side.

"No sex," I said. We kissed softly until we both fell asleep.

I woke up to the smell of eggs, bacon, and grits. I got up and walked to the kitchen. Mya still had on her boy shorts and tank, but she also had on this cute red apron that read "Kiss the Chef." I smiled, walked behind her, turned her face, and kissed her softly. She moaned softly and said good morning.

"Good morning, sexy. Is all this for me, or is this my cue to leave?" I said while taking a seat at the bar. Her hotel looked just like a two-bedroom apartment; it was crazy. The hotel room looked like it could have come from an Ikea magazine.

"If you leave, I would be so upset with you. So, take a seat, either in here or in the bed, and find something to watch. The food will be ready in about ten minutes," Mya said.

I obeyed her order, returned to bed, and flipped through channels. As always, nothing was on TV, so I listened to the music channel. I put it on the hip-hop channel and grabbed my phone:

3 missed calls

7 New Messages

"Damn." One missed call from Toni and two from Elle—four messages from Elle, two from Toni, and one from notification Twitter.

Elle 6:12 a.m.: We need to talk. I called you.

Elle 6:13 a.m.: I know you're probably mad,

but it hurt when I heard about you at the park.

I felt like you lied and led me on this entire time.

Can we talk?

Elle 7:47 a.m.: I know you're probably at work by now.

I would like to hear from you at some point today.

I'm cooking dinner. Can you come over tonight, and we can talk?

Reading Elle's text messages had me ready to drop her ass. I decided not to text her. I didn't care what she cooked. Nothing explained who was in her apartment, so everything else was irrelevant. I had nothing to say to her, and I had no plans to go there tonight. Next!

Toni texted and asked if I made it home. She also told me that Chelsea was feeling me. I thought that was weird because the entire night was spent with me venting about Elle. I didn't need any more women on my roster. I had my hands filled trying to figure out my feelings for Elle and if I could pursue what feelings were brewing for Mya. I didn't need more distractions.

I texted Toni back and told her I was good. I was going to relax at home. I pressed send. Mya walked into the room with two plates.

INTELLEGENT_ELLE

When you miss someone so bad
you do stupid sh*t to get their
attention.

"You want water, orange juice, or soda?" Mya said. She gave me one plate and put the other on the bed.

"Water." She returned from the room with two bottles of water. I turned off my phone.

Mya sat on the bed and grabbed her plate. We ate and vibe to the music.

After eating, I laid down on her thigh. She welcomed me and started playing with my hair.

"I love your hair," Mya said, messaging my scalp.

"If I tell you all the things that turn me on about you, you will think I am crazy," I said while enjoying her fingers through my scalp.

"You're just a little charmer, aren't you?" Mya said while playfully pulling my hair back, making me look into her eyes. She smiled, looking beautiful as the sun bounced off her face, making that dimple I love too much stand out.

That was it. I couldn't take it anymore. I wanted to feel her body against mine. I wanted to hear her moan. So, I turned around and got between her legs.

"What are you doing?" Mya said softly.

Instead of answering, I kissed her softly while slowly laying her on her back. She wrapped her arms around my neck and let me lead. I began to kiss her neck while rubbing her thigh. It felt like her skin melted in my hands.

She rubbed her feet on my leg and let out a soft moan. I continued to kiss her lower and lower. I pulled up her shirt over her breast. Her nipples were small and perfectly circled, staring dead at me, inviting me to put them in my mouth. How could I say no to them?

I took one of her nipples in my mouth. The warmth of my tongue made her back arch. She left off a soft moan and grabbed my ears. I took my time with each nipple, rotating my tongue around the nipple and biting them softly. Her moans grew louder as I flicked my tongue on the left nipple while slightly pinching the right.

I made my way down to her stomach. She had a little tattoo of a small dragon on her right rib. But, of course, I had to kiss that too. Every inch of her that I uncovered seemed more beautiful than the last.

I continued until I reached her belly button, kissing and licking it like it was my special area. Her moans were so sexy and seemed to motivate me.

I slowly pulled her panties down. Her sweet spot was freshly shaved, and her lips were pink and fat. I needed to taste her. I spread her legs slowly and watched her clit expose itself to me like we were having a formal introduction, and I couldn't wait to say hello with my tongue.

I hungrily dove head-first. She arched her back and let out the most erotic moan in the world like she was anticipating my tongue. She reached down and pulled up my undershirt, digging her nails into my back on the way up. I let her pull it over my head and kissed her on my way back down and kissed her swollen clit.

I lifted her ass cheeks so that her sweet spot leveled my face and devoured her as if it was the best meal I'd ever eaten. I wasn't going to stop until I felt her cum. I couldn't stop if I tried the way she held my head on her clit. She felt so good, tasted so good, and sounded so good.

"Oh my god, J. You feel so good… right there… just like that," she moaned. "Baby. Suck my clit, baby, just like that… don't stop… please don't stop. I'm about to cum."

She locked her legs behind me as I flicked and sucked her clit. I felt her juices flow down my chin. Her breathing started to pick up, and I could feel her pussy muscles contracting. I was in a zone. Her pussy, and my tongue just started a special connection. There was no way I would stop.

"Baby, baby… yesssss. Don't stop. I'm going to cum," I moaned. She grabbed my hair, pushed down on my head, and started grinding wildly. I began sucking, making slurping sounds as her body got stiff, her mouth open, then she collapsed and pushed my head away.

I kissed her down her thighs, just to give her pussy a short break because I wasn't done. She was still letting out soft moans and moving her hips when she pulled me up to her face and started kissing me softly.

Her lips were sweet, and her breathing was heavy. I moved from her lips and began sucking on her neck. She dug her nails into my back as I dry-humped her, feeling her juices on my pelvis. She wrapped her legs around my hips and matched my rhythm.

"What are you doing to me?" Mya moaned in my ear.

That only motivated me more. I moved my hand down between her legs and started circling the entrance to her sex tunnel. She exhaled softly in my ear and pulled my earlobe in her mouth. I slid my middle finger inside her, and she released a soft gasp. She was so tight and wet. I started working my finger in and out of her slowly. She moved her hips as I curved my finger upward, tickling her G-spot. Her moans grew, so I added another finger.

"Baby," she said and tilted her head back. I kissed her in the middle of her neck and slid my fingers inside her as deeply as possible. I could feel her juices in the palm of my hands.

I picked up the pace a little and started finger fucking her with my curved fingers. I continued to massage her G-spot.

"Fuck me, J… fuck me just like that, baby," Mya said through breaths.

I didn't lose my rhythm. I worked my fingers in and out of here while rubbing her clit with my thumb. Mya's juices began running down my arm. Her body began to jerk wildly with every stroke.

I felt her muscles begin to contract. Still, I didn't stop. I kept going, picking up the pace a little. Her nails dug deeper into my back, and I could hear her trying to catch her breath.

"Baby, Baby, Baby, Baby," repeated. Then, her pussy muscles started going crazy, and all I heard was silence. Mya's head tilted back and her mouth open, but no sound escaped.

Mya's whole body dropped down on the bed. She grabbed my hand, pushed my finger inside as deep as they could go, rotated her hips a few times, and quickly pulled me out.

"I can't take anymore. But you feel so good," she said.

I went back down and licked the juices off her thighs to her pussy. I stuck my tongue inside of her. I wanted to taste all that I had drained from her body. She arched her back and opened her legs further, letting my tongue easily slip into her hole. I stuck the two fingers back inside her pussy, pulled out, and stuck them into her mouth. She welcomed the taste and slid her tongue between my fingers. I crawled back up and kissed her deeply, pushing my tongue into her mouth. She slowly pushed me off her and walked to the bathroom.

I heard her turn on the shower and stood at the entrance. I admired every inch of her body and could still smell and taste her on my lips.

"Are you coming?" she said, placing her hands on her naked hips.

"Hell yeah," I said, smiling, jumping out of bed.

In the shower together, we rubbed and kissed all over each other. I washed her thoroughly from head to toe, and she returned the favor.

"Are you going to tell me what happened last night?" Mya asked. She was standing behind me, helping wash the suds off my back.

"What do you mean?" I asked.

"You called me at two in the morning, drunk, and you seemed upset," she said.

"What makes you think I was upset?" I said.

"You get quiet and stare off when something is bothering you. Plus, you stormed in last night as if you were upset," she said.

"I was a little upset, but nothing you couldn't cure with your presence," I said.

"Okay. Are you ready to get out?" Mya asked.

"Yeah."

After the shower, I put on my clothes, and Mya walked me to the door.

"So, am I going to see you today?" I asked her, pulling her close to me.

"If you want to. I'm free later, and honestly, I would love to see you again," Mya said.

"I'm off all day today, so just let me know when I can come back over," I said, kissing her on the cheeks.

"Ok," she said, wrapping her arms around my neck. After a few minutes of kissing, we finally pulled apart and said goodbye.

Chapter Nine

When I got in my truck, I called Toni, and she picked up on the third ring.

"What up, bro. You trying to chill tonight?" Toni said.

I was ready to open up about Mya about her. I wanted to see Mya more, and I was feeling her. I planned on spending more time with her while she was here, and I didn't want to tip-toe around Toni. As far as I was concerned, Elle and I were done and over. I know she has always been "team Elle," but it's time to end that chapter. Plus, I wanted to talk about my night with my bro about my crazy ass night.

"Bro, man, I got to talk to you. Shit has been crazy since I left your spot last night," I said.

"What happened? Hold on, let me go outside really quick." I could hear her moving around as if her phone was in her pocket. "Alright, my bad. I had to light one, this shit might be funny," She continued.

"When I left your apartment, I drove to Elle's to talk and figure this shit out. She opened the door and stepped into the hallway," I said.

"The hallway?"

"Yeah, the hallway. I figured Elle was mad, so I let it slide, but in the middle of our conversation, I heard someone coughing in the background," I said.

"So, she had another bitch up in her crib?" she replied.

"After hearing whoever that was, she ran into the house and closed the door in my face," I said.

"Damn, I wish I was there! We would have bussed that door open and snatched her ass up. So, what did you do? You just left?" Toni said.

"Yeah, I left. I'm done with Elle's ass after that bullshit. To think I was going over there to fix the shit, and she had another bitch in there."

"That would fuck me up to," she said.

"We are done, man. I don't even want to talk to her. She has been calling me all day and texting, but I'm not fucking with her ass no more," I said.

"Why are you just now telling me this? It's almost noon?" Toni said.

"You remember the lady house we did the kitchen for a few months back? She wasn't home, and her daughter...."

"Yeah, I remember her. the one with the fine ass daughter, " she said.

"Yeah, with the fine ass daughter. We exchanged numbers that day and have been talking back and forth. After what happened with Elle, I hit her up last night and chilled with her," I said. There was a brief silence on the phone, and I could hear Toni puffing on the blunt.

So, you're moving on to Mya?" Toni said. I was completely caught off guard hearing Mya's name. I never said, and I didn't think Toni would remember her like that.

"It's not like that. We just texted now and then and talked every blue moon, but yesterday was the first time we chilled," I lied. There was another long pause.

"Yeah. Well, hit me up if you still want to chill later," Toni said and ended the call.

This girl sleeps with every woman that walks past her, but if one of them shows me interest and not her, she acts like I took the love of her life, just like what happened with this girl named Erica.

Erica was this girl who lived and worked in our dorm as a resident assistant. Toni had a crush on her, but she couldn't stand Toni. At the time, Toni and I had been friends for about a year but had become more like sisters. We went everywhere together and even picked the same classes that year.

Erica was a junior, while Toni and I were both sophomores. I knew that Toni liked Erica, but Erica never gave her any play because she said Toni acted too young. Every time Toni saw Erica working at the front desk, Toni would chill in the lobby, being loud and flirting with her and every girl who walked through the door. Then, she would lean on Erica's post and tell everyone how Erica would be hers one day.

Well, that day never happened. Instead, one night, I was walking back from the campus store, and Erica drove by asking me if I wanted a ride to the dorm. I gladly accepted because it was already dark, and I was alone. Instead of going to the dorm room, we talked at the practice football field's bleachers.

I never looked at Erica like that because Toni was my friend. I believed in loyalty before females and still believe in that today. Even when she mentioned Toni, I tried to make her sound good. But I couldn't make Toni look any better. Toni was a player, and she didn't care. Toni stayed, running after anyone she thought was gay. Hell, that was damn near ran through every girl on campus. Erica just happened to be a challenge, and she loved that.

Erica told me that night she would never talk to Toni. She said Toni wasn't her type. Come to find out, Erica was feeling me and wanted to get to know me. Erica explained that she never said anything because Toni always tried to flirt, even when she asked about me. I admitted that Toni never told me she asked about me, and she wasn't surprised. That night, we just talked and laughed until about one in the morning.

When I returned to the dorm, Toni was sitting in the lobby with other people, talking and joking. Erica and I didn't say anything when we entered. Erica walked to the elevator, and I went to see what Toni was up to. After questioning why she saw me with Erica, Toni stopped talking to me for weeks.

I couldn't help that she was feeling me and didn't want Toni. I didn't want to go there with Erica anyway. When Erica finally got the picture that I considered her a friend, she started messing with Toni. I don't know if it was to make me mad or jealous, but I didn't care. Eventually, Toni began talking to me, only to brag about finally sleeping with Erica. But I didn't care.

My phone began ringing, interrupting my thoughts. I knew it was Elle from the ringtone, so I pressed the ignore button without looking down. I didn't feel like arguing with her. Plus, I was still on a

Mya high. Elle called back, and I sent her to voicemail... again.

Toni

I can't believe she felt the need not to tell me about Mya, like it's a secret or something. I don't want that girl. I holla at everybody, that hoe aint special. The only reason why she wanted to fuck with Mya in the first place was because she saw me trying to talk to her.

It's always something sneaky with her ass. I don't know why she thinks she is better than me. She loves to talk about the women I date, but as soon as she sees me talking to someone, she goes behind my back and tries to take them. J is my friend but tends to act like she's better than me.

We brought our business from the ground up, together, but she always seemed to think she did it alone. She likes to forget that it was my connection that got us that business loan and if it wasn't for me, she would still be miserable at her parents' house.

Because of me, she lives in the city and looks down on everybody, thinking she is all high and mighty. But she ain't nobody. Fuck her! I make the same amount of money as her, but she thinks she is beneath me for some reason.

I reached for the half-smoked joint sitting in the ashtray. As soon as I inhaled, my doorbell rang.

"Who is it?" I yelled from my sofa.

"Elle! Is J over here?" I heard her say through the door. I Jumped up, sat the joint in the ashtray, and ran to the door. Before I opened the door, I adjusted my shirt, fixed my cargo shorts, and pulled my locs to the front.

"What's up, Elle?" I said, opening the door.

"I've been calling her all night and morning. I know she told you what went down last night, but it wasn't even like that," Elle said, storming into my apartment.

Elle wore short jeans and a blue crop top that stopped above her belly button. Her long hair was straightened and combed to one side of her head. I couldn't lie. Elle was fine as fuck. But Elle is the type of woman who spends her Saturday morning at the salon, then at the nail shop or spa. Then she probably stopped by somewhere like Chipotle and picked up lunch with her girlfriends. Elle was a bill. J doesn't mind paying for all of that. I was not. She is too damn bougie for me.

"Yeah, she told me what happened last night. That was some foul shit. How are you going to have another female in there?" I said like I cared about their relationship. I didn't.

"I was trying to make her jealous. It was just a friend, and we were watching movies." Elle sashed past me and sat on the couch as if she knew I was watching her, teasing me with her wide hips and fat ass. "I don't know why I came here like this, but she's not answering my calls. Maybe you can talk to her for me," Elle said.

I didn't see why she liked J so much. I mean, J is cute. But cute, like a puppy. She needed to taste this Pitbull and watch it change her life.

"I know she trips sometimes, but she cares about you, " I said.

"I hope you're right, Toni," Elle said.

"Do you know anything about her being at the park the other day with some girl?" Elle asked.

"No, she told me she was hanging with you? She was here last night but left a little after one, " I said.

"I dove by her place earlier and didn't see her car in the parking lot," she said.

"I don't know anything about that. She called me not that long ago, but that was to tell me what happened. She did sound like she was the car, though," I said.

"So, she didn't go home last night," she said.

"I guess not."

"Wait! What the hell am I mad for? She fucked up, I just returned the favor by hanging with my ex." She spoke.

Elle stood up, put her hands on her hip, and bent one leg to the side. Elle may have had a good job and lived in the city, but she couldn't hide the hood in her. I can see it in her body language. I was determined to bring it out of her. If I know the hood version of Elle, she might be worth my time.

"J is still my bro, so that's fucked up," I said. J acted as if she was sent from God himself, but now I see she is sneaky as hell.

"Yeah, I'm sure it's over now," she said.

"I can tell you that she was coming to talk to you and make up. So, I'm pretty sure she is beyond pissed after seeing someone in your condo. But honestly, I would have done the same thing if I were you. But you didn't hear it from me," I said, giving her my million-dollar smile and wink.

She smiled, turned away, and exited the apartment. I followed Elle to the door, watching her ass move with every step. She was crazy sexy, and I know I was wrong, but I low-key wanted to see how that ass felt.

I smiled at the thought and closed the door. J straight up lied to me about being with Elle the other day. She was probably with Mya, but why would she hide that? I know she doesn't think I wanted her ass. I might have tried to get her number when we were at her house, but I tried to get everybody's number. That hoe wasn't special.

I know too many females like Mya. She thinks she's all high and mighty. She was probably the only child and loved by both of her parents. I could see her being the golden child with all her ugly drawings on the refrigerator or locked up in a box along with her tricycle she had at three. Mya isn't my type.

J loves to say I only talk to hood females, but that's not true. I'll holla at anybody as long as they're fine. My strap doesn't discriminate, nor does it have income restrictions. If a fine female wants to ride it, I will saddle up. Females from my side of town are just easy to bag.

I'm a player like my pops. Don't get me wrong, my pops love my mom, but when you're the biggest dealer in the streets, women throw that pussy at you left and right. My mom understood the game. One thing about my pop, though, is he never let any female disrespect my mom's. They were a quick fuck, and he made that be known. My mom was his heart, and the females were just easy bodies. I guess that's how I felt, too, except no woman has ever had my heart.

Chapter Ten

J

It was still early, and I had nothing planned for the day. Mya had worn my ass out that I went home and crashed. It was after six before I woke up. I immediately turned my phone on silent. I wanted some peace. I wanted to avoid hearing from Elle. The way Toni sounded on the phone, I wasn't too eager to call her either. I had already made up my mind that I would spend the day to myself. We had a busy schedule tomorrow, so I would deal with her attitude then. I really wanted to chill in my apartment and talk to Mya tonight.

After rubbing the sleep out of my eyes, I unlocked my phone. I had three new text messages and one missed call. The call was from my mother. I made a mental note to call her tomorrow. I was serious about not wanting to talk to anyone but Mya. She seemed like the only person in my life not surrounded by drama. Plus, I knew my mom only wanted money.

Ever since we started making real money, it seemed like she called me every other weekend for cash. My dad retired recently and hasn't been able to keep up with my mom's lavish lifestyle, so I've been her financer for the past four months. Lately, she's been wanting more and more, and now, I ignore her calls.

The text from Elle telling me that she would no longer contact me was like music to my ear. After the stunt she pulled, there was no way I could come back from that. I shouldn't be mad because of Mya, but I would have never disrespected her that way. I know I may have been up and down with my feelings, but I always gave her the utmost respect.

Mya: Me…you….dvd…pizza?

The message from Mya pushed Elle out of my mind. I immediately texted her back, telling her I was down and would even order the pizza. The last notification was a direct Twitter message from Elle asking if I was avoiding her. Again, I ignored her. Plus, I had a date.

Mya said she would be over at 8 p.m. It was 6:45. I needed to shower and order the pizza. I was happy that Mya hit me up. I was already picturing her and me cuddling, eating pizza, and watching movies. I don't know what it was about her, but I was beginning to love every minute with her.

I laid my purple and turquoise Jordan basketball shorts and a white wife beater on the bed. I got some Jordan socks, put the matching purple and turquoise hat on top, and grabbed my towel off the door.

I hopped in the shower and tried to clear my mind while the hot water ran down my back. I couldn't relax, though. My mind was on overdrive. I thought about Elle and how much I liked her. I never thought that we wouldn't end this way. At one point, I thought my ex-wife and how I thought our divorce was the universe pushing us apart so that I could meet Elle like fate led me to her. But then, it was like Elle changed within the last few months, and I began to see sides of her. Necessarily, I was not too fond of her insecure ways. It's not all on her, though. I may have changed since meeting Mya.

Is it my fault for how things turned out? I could go and talk to Elle and work out our issues, but did I want to? Did I want to be with Elle, or was I just comfortable with where we were? Was I ready to commit to her? Then there is Mya. It's something about her that is drawing me to her. Her smile. The way she lit up a room. Even before she came into town, our conversations were so deep. I had told Mya things I'd never admitted to Elle. Mya takes me to a level of vulnerability that I never experienced. Until I figured things out, keeping Elle at a distance was best. Plus, it gave me room to explore things with Mya.

The more I thought about it, the more I realized I needed to give Elle her space. I didn't want to lead her on any more than I had. I didn't want a relationship with her. I was content with what we had, nothing more. I guess you could say that I chose Mya. Even though Elle and I weren't in a relationship, why did it still feel wrong?

I turned the shower off and stepped out. I wrapped the towel around me and pulled my hair into a bun. I quickly changed my mind and started to braid it into two braids just in case it got wild between us. I'm learning that Mya is a hairpuller, and I didn't want to wake up early to straighten it.

Once done, I put on my clothes and ordered the pizza. I walked into the living room to sit on the couch. Mya would be there any moment, so I flicked on the music channels, leaned my head back on the sofa, and listened to the sweet sound of Usher while I waited.

It was 8:03 when I heard a knock at the door and immediately got excited. I got up and looked through the peephole. I could see Mya smiling with a bag in her hands. I opened the door and was greeted with a tight hug.

"Hey baby girl, I'm glad you're here," I said.

"I had some time on my hand, so I decided to spend it with you," she said while playfully hitting me in my stomach.

"I'm glad you can fit me into your schedule. Was the place hard to find?" I said.

"No, my GPS led me straight here. I got wine!" She held up a bottle. "I figured we couldn't have pizza without wine. Oh, and I bought my favorite scary movie," she said.

"We can't just Netflix and chill like regular people?" I asked.

"Don't tell me you don't have a DVD player," she said.

"I surprisingly do. It came with the surround sound," I said.

"Netflix is cool, but how can you beat this classic," she said, holding up a copy of the original Candyman.

"Yo, this is what we're watching? I love that movie," I said.

I sat the bags on the counter, and Mya wrapped her hands around my waist. I turned around and kissed her forehead.

"Hi," she said.

"Hi." I kissed Mya on her cheek, and she hugged me.

"Are you ready for this?" she said, holding the movie up again.

"You or the movie?" I said.

"Both," Mya said.

"I'm ready for everything," I said.

"I bet. So, where are your glasses? Mya said, breaking our hold.

"I got you," I said, reaching for the glasses and sitting them on the counter. I grabbed the wine opener and proceeded to open the bottle.

"Did the front desk give you any problems when you came up?" I asked her, pouring the wine into our glasses.

"No, once I gave them my I.D., they let me right up," she said.

"Good. Let me give you the tour," I said, handing her the glass of wine.

I walked her through the living room and bedroom. My apartment was small, so the tour ended rather quickly. I always dreamed of living in the heart of Atlanta above shops. When I got the opportunity, I did just that. After showing her where the bathroom was, we sat on the couch, talked a little, and waited for the pizza.

Two glasses of wine and 40 minutes later, the pizza arrived. I grabbed the pizza from the door, signed the receipt, and closed the door. When I got to the couch, Mya had begun the movie. I put the box in the middle of the table, sat beside Mya, and wrapped my arm around her. As if the spot belonged to her, she curled her feet up on the couch and rested her head under her arm. I reached down with my free hand and grabbed us both a slice of pizza.

"If you're scared, don't worry. I got you," I said, kissing her curly hair.

"Honestly, I'm not a big scary movie fan," she said.

"So, why did you choose this movie?"

"So, I could do this," she said, wrapping her arms around my waist and squeezing me.

"I could do this watching a Disney movie," I said. She looked up, smiled, and kissed me on the lip before taking a bite of pizza.

"Just hold me during the scary parts," she said with a mouth full of pizza.

"I got you," I said, taking a bite.

After eating a few slices and closing the box, Mya got up, and I laid on my back. She got between my legs and put her head on my chest. She was comfortable with me, and I enjoyed her body and presence. It felt like we'd known each other for years. I grabbed the folded throw blanket in the chair and spread it over us.

Music began to play whenever it got quiet or suspenseful, and she hid under the covers. I fought with her to make her watch, and she screamed that she didn't want to see it. I would laugh, and she would playfully hit me on my arm. Eventually, the movie ended, and it felt like the feeling you have when you come home from a vacation. You're sad it's over and wish it lasted one more day.

"I haven't watched this movie in so long. I got from an old stash at my mom's," she said.

"Although you missed about seventy-five percent of it under the covers," I said.

"Whatever, I felt you jumping too," she replied, squeezing my knee.

"Come here," I said, sitting up and pulling her between my legs. She sat with her back against my chest, and I rested my face between her neck and shoulders. She held my head and leaned back until we were face to face.

We stared at each other, and it felt like the world had gotten still. Even the movie silenced in the background, it seemed. We kissed slowly and sexually. Until we both jumped from a knock at the door. We looked at each other, confused. I wasn't expecting anyone else, and I didn't tell the front desk to let anyone up.

"Are you expecting someone?" Mya asked.

"No!" I grabbed the remote and muted the TV. I didn't know who was at my door, but I prayed it wasn't Elle. She and Toni was the only person I could think about that could get through security without them having to call for permission, but I damn sure didn't put her on the guest list today.

I looked out the peephole and saw Toni. Thank God it wasn't Elle. I made a mental note to take them off my frequent visitor list.

I opened the door, and Toni walked in as if she lived there. I quickly put aside the brewing irritable feeling and closed the door behind her. Since our dry conversation on the phone, she was the last person I wanted to see. Well, second to last.

"Man, I have been calling you all day," she said. That was a lie. I am still waiting to have one missed call or text from her. I have avoided Elle all day, though.

"I'm just chilling, man. Enjoying our day off. I don't have a missed call from you," I said dryly, watching her almost break her neck to see who was sitting on the couch. Mya had her back facing the door, playing on her phone.

"Toni, you remember Mya, right?" I said.

"Yeah, I remember her," Toni said. She walked to the side of the couch, never taking her eyes off Mya.

"Are you going to sit down?" Toni sucked her teeth, still eyeing Mya. Mya looked at me and pulled the cover over her body. I could tell she was uncomfortable, and I couldn't blame her. Toni was starting to get on my nerves more and more every day.

"So, what's up, Toni? What do you want?" I said.

"Nothing, just trying to see what you're into, and now I know. I will see you tomorrow at work. I don't want to interrupt what you got going on," Toni said with a devilish smile. She started walking to the door. I got up quickly to let her out. "Well, good night."

"Yep," I said, following her and closing the door as soon as her feet crossed the doorway. I walked back over to Mya and slowly slid the cover off her.

"I'm sorry. I don't know why she came here," I said, rubbing Mya's thigh to ease the tension.

"Your friend is creepy," Mya said.

"I don't know what her problem has been lately. She has been acting weird the last few days," I said. "Let's not let it ruin our night."

She let out a sigh and pulled me up to her face. She kissed the tip of my nose and then my lips. One small peck to the lips turned into a passionate kiss.

Before I knew it, I lifted her and guided her to my bedroom.

She relaxed and arched her back as I undressed her and moaned in my ear whenever my hands contacted her skin as if she were trained to speak with my every touch. I guided her to the edge of the bed and got on my knees. I put my hands under her buttocks and lifted her to my face.

I kissed each thigh softly, using my full lips, not just a peck. I made my way down her thigh and stopped the moment my lips grazed her lower lips. I softly kissed her clit that was peeking through her slits. She inhaled quickly, rotating her hips. I slide my tongue deep inside her, feeling her pussy contract. Pulling out, I sucked her clit, slurping and flicking her swollen button. Her hand gripped my head, pushing me deeper into her slits. I ate her pussy like a sweet watermelon on a hot date. She began to rotate wildly, so I gripped her ass cheeks tighter and held on tight. Then her body froze, and her mouth opened, but no sound escaped. I flicked and licked her click, making circles with my tongue, and slurping sounds with my mouth. Her grip tightened.

Toni

I only went over there to tell her what happened with Elle. I couldn't believe she tried me like that. Both of them are sitting and looking at me like I'm a fucking crazy or something. Talking to me like I was not shit. I swear she thinks her shit doesn't stink. Fuck her.

Every time J is in front of a female, she acts differently as fuck. I remember one time in college with this girl, Erica. J knew I was trying to bag her, but she went behind me and started hanging with her on the low. Suddenly, she didn't want anything to do with me.

I know J was talking behind my back, but I let it go. I eventually secured the bag and even turned her against J. I still remember the look on J's face when she saw her walking out of my door room. She knew what was up.

I was getting tired of J, and someone needed to kick her off this high horse she felt she was riding on.

Just as I opened my car door, a thought came into my head. So, I started my car and headed to Elle's condo.

"Who is it?" I said, sounding like she was getting out of bed. I could hear the squeaking from the mattress and her stumbling to the door. I don't see how they live in these little ass apartments. If I wanted to be downtown, I'd rent a room or something. They actually live in these designer storage boxes.

"It's Toni. Is J over here?" I said, already knowing the answer.

Elle opened the door, looking like she hadn't slept in days. Her shorts and a tank top were covered in food stains, and her hair was still in a bonnet. She had dark circles around her eyes and smelled of whiskey. But, even then, she still was sexy as fuck.

"No, I haven't talked to your friend since that night," Elle said, letting me inside.

"I texted her earlier and told her I was done stalking her ass. She texted me back hours later and said cool." She said while sitting on her sofa.

I noticed the defeated look on her face. "I'm just over it," she said.

"I saw her earlier, and she said we would chill tonight, but now she's M.I.A. I went to her house and could have sworn I heard the T.V. on, but she never answered the door. I called her phone, but it went straight to voicemail," I lied. "I thought maybe she was over here."

"She's probably with that bitch and didn't want to answer the door. I swear I hate your fucking friend. I hope she found what she wanted," she said, as if it hurt for those words to leave her mouth.

"I told her she needs to be straight with you, but she wasn't trying to hear all that. That girl must have her head gone because she is tripping hard," I said.

When I said something about Mya, I hit a nerve because her eyes began to puff back up. I wanted to see how far I could get.

"She hasn't even been in town that long, and she is already changing," I said.

She put her head in her hands, and I could see the tears running down Elle's face. It still trips me out that J pulled Elle's old ass. She ain't that old, but she's older by a lot. She's beautiful, though, and paid. Elle is jealous as fuck and a little crazy if you ask me.

"She's been in town for about five days, huh? I know this because that's when J started acting differently towards me. All of a sudden, she needed space," Elle said.

"I believe so," I admitted. At least that much I thought was true. Before that, I noticed that she constantly texted while we were at work. I automatically thought it was Elle.

"I knew not to get my feelings involved. My friends told me not to fuck with her. I should have listened to them. For months, I've been feeling like something has been going on. I've been trying to figure out why she was changing for months. But she kept making it seem like I was pressuring her and tripping. The whole time, she was entertaining someone else," she said.

I got up and sat next to her. I smiled as I wrapped my arms around her shoulders and pulled her close. She began to cry.

"Elle, you're a real ass woman and deserve more. She is fucking up, and instead of being real, she's been shady. Let her do her. But don't be over here crying your heart out. You're worth more than that," I said.

I kissed her cheek softly and wiped a tear away with my free hand. She wrapped her arms around my waist, pulling me closer. I let her cry, and when she stopped crying, I kissed her forehead and let her know it was going to be alright.

"Your friend should be here right now, not you, Toni. So why are you here and she's not?" Elle said.

"I mean, I came to look for J, but I see you're hurting, so I can stay as long as you need me," I said, hugging her tighter.

What a lame ass line. That's some shit J would say. All this damn crying was irritating the hell out of me.

Elle smiled and kissed me on the cheek. I kissed her on the forehead and lifted her chin so that she could see my face.

"You're better than this, and you deserve better," I said, licking my lips. I was on a role.

Elle stared into my eyes as if she was trying to see if I was serious, but little did she know, my game face had always been solid. I watched as her eyes left my eyes and moved down to my lips. I licked them slowly and smiled.

"Okay, you have to get up out of here. It's getting late, and I have to be up early," Elle said, getting up off the couch. She grabbed my hand and led me to the door. I playfully pulled back as if I didn't want to leave. If she really wanted me to, I would stay.

Elle hesitated for a moment. I saw it.

"Yeah, you're right, but I can write my number down. Text or call me whenever you want to talk or whatever", I said.

"Okay," Elle said. She grabbed her purse, reached inside, and grabbed a pen and an old receipt. Elle handed me both and continued to the door.

"You're too pretty to be crying. Get some rest and hit me up tomorrow. We can hang out and get your mind off things," I said, handing her the pen and a receipt after writing my number on the back. Once at the door, I hugged Elle, but this time I squeezed her extra tight so I could feel them big ass titties.

"I'll think about it," Elle said.

I left Elle's apartment feeling better. J is my friend, but my dad taught me that family is the only people you can trust and keep everybody else at a distance. Family was all we had, and we made sure that we stuck together.

When my dad got locked up, my mom fell into a deep depression and started drinking and doing drugs. She changed so much so quick that by the end of the year, you could barely recognize her. My dad tried his hardest to get her help. He may have still had the streets on lock, but controlling my mother from behind bars was a different battle. She died when I was ten. It was my brother K.J. who stepped up and took care of me.

Keon Jr was the spitting image of my dad, only lighter. He took the completion of my mother. My sexy chocolate ass complimented my father.

Not too long after my father got locked up, my brother took over the family business while our dad was doing life behind bars.

K.J. was fifteen when our mom died. We lived with our grandma in the suburbs but kept the family business alive. I remember K.J. always being gone the first two years we moved in. Uncle Bo, one of my father's right hands, would pick him up and be gone for days. He trained my brother under my father's orders.

I begged my brother to put me on when I came of age, but he never would. He would take me on his runs, and I ate everything up. But K.J., my father, and Uncle Bo were persistent about me being better. They loved to say that they wanted better for me.

Growing up, I did what I was told, kept my grades up, and graduated. After that, I went to college, got a degree, and started a business, but the streets always stayed on me. I never needed K.J. or none of them to put me on. I've been slanging since middle school, everything from candy to weed. I'm my father's daughter, hands down.

When I was sixteen, my brother caught me selling at school. My brother was twenty-one then, and my grandmother was probably passed out somewhere at a bar. My mother didn't fall far from the tree. She ended up being a drunk, too.

I got caught selling because of a surprise locker inspection. The police came and locked me up. Of course, my brother showed up and saved the day. Because of my family's reputation and money, I got all charges dropped and a second chance. I got so much play after that at school. I didn't need my family's name. I had begun to build my own reputation.

When I got home that day, my brother took one of my father's thick leather belts and beat me until I was black and blue, per my dad's orders. From that moment on, I never got caught dealing again. I just got better at hiding it.

I became the perfect student after that. I pulled my grades up and used my new platform to keep the drugs out of my hands. I hired a few of my homeboys to hold and supply the students while concentrating on good grades. The good thing was that the better my grades got, the more my dad and brother spoiled me. They never questioned me again.

When I got accepted to FAMU, my family was so proud. Although I wouldn't say I liked school because I would rather be in the streets watching over my brother. Instead, I followed my father's plan for me.

If it wasn't for J, I would have probably failed. Once I realized she was smart, I kept her close and changed my classes and degree to what she was pursuing. While she was busy studying and attending our classes, I chased females in the streets.

When I told my dad about starting a business with my degree, he was so happy that he put in a good word with a bank manager on our payroll to give us a nice-sized business loan. J took over from there while I still chased after hoes. She basically handles everything while I show up when I want to do whatever I want. Business was good even though it was just another source of income for me. Like I said, I've been hustling since middle school.

Chapter Eleven
(The Next Morning)

I was lying with my head tilted back. Mya was between my thighs, caressing my leg with one hand and rubbing my clit with the thumb of her other hand. My moans grew louder as I held my breast in my hands, squeezing my nipples between my fingers and gripping my breast.

She grabbed my legs and spread them wider, sucking and flicking on my button. I let out a loud gasp and grabbed the back of her head. I started grinding slowly on her face, pushing her harder. I could hear moaning, and it turned me on even more.

Twenty minutes and two orgasms later, we were sitting naked with her on my lap and her legs wrapped around my waist, kissing passionately. I grabbed her, picked her up, and carried her to the shower. I washed her, and she returned the favor, making sure not to miss a spot. An hour later, we were dressed and ready to start our day.

I walked Mya to her car. When we reached her car, I turned her around and wrapped her arms around my neck. She held on tight and kissed me on my cheek.

"Text me later or call me when you get home," she said.

"Of course. Will I see you tonight?" I said.

"I was hoping you asked," she said while playfully tugging my shirt. I love it when she rubs on me and continuously places kisses anywhere that she can reach. My love language is physical touch, and she loves it. "I would love to."

I gave her a kiss on the lip and opened her door. She stepped in, started her car, and let down the window. I reached in and kissed her again. I didn't want her to leave. I wanted to stay home and cuddle all day. My stomach still hurts from the constant laughing and joking all night. I enjoyed having her around.

"I'll call you," I told her, giving her one last kiss.

"You better," she said as she backed up slowly and pulled off. As soon as she was out of sight, I checked the time. Fuck! I was going to be late. I ran to my car, pulled the address into my GPS, and hopped on the road. It was already 8:45, and 9 p.m. was our arrival time. I had to be in Marietta within 15 minutes. I clearly was looking for a miracle during Atlanta's morning traffic.

I arrived at the client's house and saw our work truck parked. I figured Toni had gotten the car and driven there when she realized I was running late. That was the plan that we both agreed on. We would not sit in the garage and wait if one was running late. We would take the work truck, go to the customer's house, and meet there. It was better than arriving late to the customers trying to wait on each other. Usually, it's me arriving early and Toni eventually popping up with an excuse for why she was late.

"Your colleague told me that she was expecting you. I'll show you to the kitchen," The homeowner said and escorted me inside.

"Thank you," I said.

When I walked into the kitchen, Toni had already torn everything down. She nodded at me and continued to rip out the last old cabinets. That was her favorite part of the job. When she was irate, she would grab the sledgehammer, turn on headphones, and go to work, knocking and kicking down cabinets. I just stayed out of her way.

I caught the shade, got out my phone, put on my favorite playlist, a mixture of slow music, and started dragging out the debris. I wanted to ask Toni why she popped up at my condo last night, but I let it go. I just wanted to get this day over with and go back home.

When lunchtime came, without saying anything, Toni grabbed her lunch bag and left. Usually, we would eat together, but I wasn't feeling Toni or her weird vibe. Because I didn't think to pack a lunch after my morning with Mya, I hopped in my car, drove to the nearest drive-thru, grabbed some lunch, and ate in my car.

Me: I can't lie. I would rather be with you right now.

Mya: I was thinking about you too. Stay focused so that you can finish and get back to me.

Me: I'm on lunch.

Mya: Well, in that case, I can still taste you on my lips.

Me: I can still feel your fingers inside me. I'm going to get you back, TRUST! lol

Mya: lol! We will see about that.

Me: We will! Okay, let me get back and get this day over with. I'll see you soon!

I wasn't a touch me not, like Toni. She always said it was gay, and she doesn't do that gay shit. I like a little head here and there, but my wife was a pillow princess and only went down on me a few times. Elle could be too aggressive sometimes, and that turned me off that after a while, our sex-life eventually became one-sided.

The thing I love about Mya is that I thought she was a total feminine lesbian, but I found out that morning that she considered herself a dominant fem and loved to top. That's all new to me, but I loved it there!

It was at 7 in the afternoon before we decided to call it a day. It was a big project that would take a few days to complete. We had ordered a storage unit to store the delivered materials and were packing and cleaning for the day. However, we still had to go and pick up the appliances so that we could install them all tomorrow.

Toni and I hadn't said two words to each other all day. I didn't understand her problem with me, but I wouldn't be the first to break the ice. We were better than that, but Toni's pride always took over her better judgment. I was at the point where I didn't want to deal with her attitude anymore. I noticed a pattern. Every time I met someone new, it was the same. She gets upset with me, and we fall out.

I was more than happy when we began packing up for the day. After loading everything up, I removed my headphones and turned to Toni.

"You want me to follow you to go get the appliances? How do you want to do this?" I asked her as she walked past me and got in the truck.

Her phone began to ring. Instead of answering my question, she smiled and held her finger up. I shifted my feet as I waited. I was annoyed, but it was late, and I was tired. I didn't feel like going there with Toni, but my patience started to wear out.

"What up, Miss Lady?" Toni said to whoever was on the other line, ignoring me.

I was angry because she didn't know where to pick them up. If she wanted to go alone, she would need the address. Everything in me wanted to leave her ass, hop in my truck, and go home, but I worked too hard to get this business up, and our reputation was essential to me.

"Yeah, I can meet you there. How about nine?" She said into the phone set. "Yeah, we're finishing up now. I have to go pick up some shit for tomorrow, then I could be on my way," she said and looked at me.

At this point, I was beyond pissed. I would have gone off on her without us being in the client's driveway. I knew right then that I needed to go off on my own. I was starting to see through Toni. So, instead of causing a scene, I texted her the address and walked away. She could pick it up herself.

"Nope, and I don't care," she said to the person, looked at her phone, and closed the door. Then, she started the truck and drove off. I was okay with that because she was beginning to get on my nerves.

I walked to my truck, took out my phone, and called Mya. She picked up on the second ring.

"Hey baby, hold on for a second," she said as soon as she picked up. I said OKAY and got in my truck. I drove off and connected my phone to my car speaker. I heard Mya talking to someone about a trip and how she didn't want to go. About 2 minutes later, she got back on the phone.

"Hey, sorry about that. How was work?" Mya asked, sounding excited.

"It was quiet. Toni didn't say anything to me the whole day, and to make things worse, when we were packing up, she got a phone call while I was trying to give her the address to the place to pick up the things we needed and started the conversation like I wasn't standing there. Then she got on the phone, and I knew she was talking about me right in my face," I rambled.

"First of all, calm down and breathe between your sentences," Mya said.

I took a deep breath. "It's just been a long day. Toni didn't make it any easier. I'm tired of dealing with her mood swings," I said.

"I know you love her best friend, but I don't get a good vibe from her. She is trouble," she said.

"No, she's cool. She does have issues, though. I'm not even worried about her right now. I want to collect this money for this job and take a much-needed vacation. I was thinking of going home and visiting my family for a few days to get away," I said.

I have been thinking about that a lot. Especially since the fallout with Elle and me, I wanted to get away from it all. There was too much going on in my life, and the people whom I thought I could confide in, I felt like they were slowly drifting away and causing drama on the way out. Plus, my mom had been blowing up my phone all week, pretending she missed me when I knew she only wanted money. Still, I missed her, although I've been avoiding her calls.

I can admit Mya's visit threw me off. I was happy I had decided to surprise my mom, so she wasn't expecting me to show up. Since Mya touched down, we've spent every day together. For once, I was smiling, and it's been genuine. I knew she was leaving eventually, but I wanted that feeling to last as long as it could because when she hopped back on the plane, life would suck again. At least that's how I felt.

"Speaking of vacations, you know I'm a photographer in my spare time. Well, I got an invitation to shoot a wedding. The wedding is in Myrtle Beach, and it's this weekend," Mya said.

"That's great!" I wanted to be happy for her, but I also wanted to spend as much time with her as possible, especially since tomorrow was my last day at work. I guess visiting my mom was back on the table.

"I don't know about it, though. I've never done anything this big. I guess I'm just nervous. What do you think?" Mya said.

"I saw a bunch of cameras at your hotel, but I didn't know you were that into photography, too."

"Yeah, it's been more of a hobby. That's why I want to move somewhere near Piedmont Park. I love the area and could walk through the park and snap my heart away," she said. I could hear the happiness in her voice. It may be just a hobby, but I could feel her passion through her words when she talked about her art.

"You know what, just hearing you talk about photography helps me understand you. You see the beauty in the most infested parts of Atlanta. You see them with such beauty and curiosity. You are truly one of a kind, and I honestly want to know more about you," I said. "So, yes! I think you would be a great wedding photographer."

"See, you understand. Looking through the lens, I can see a person's life story. The camera catches it all. All the emotion, all the hurt, and even all the love," she said excitedly.

"I think you should do the wedding. It doesn't matter what you take a photo of. You have an eye for beauty. I said, " I think you will do better than anyone else they hire," I said. "So, why don't you study photography in college if that's what you love?"

"My parents said that it wasn't a career, and if they were going to pay for college, it would be for something I could make a living off. So, I'm majoring in accounting. Oh, my Gosh, I can't believe I'm telling you this," she said.

"I'm just happy that you feel comfortable enough to tell me. I love that you're still doing what you love on the side. You might become one of the biggest photographers and never have to use your degree," I said.

"You might be right. So, if I do the wedding, you said you need a vacation, right? You should come with me. It's only for the weekend, and it's the beach! Who can say no to the beach," she said. I could hear her smiling through my speakers.

"Now, who needs to breathe between sentences," I said.

I would love to spend time on the beach with Mya. It's only been a few days, but she was starting to become special to me, and seeing her in a bathing suit had me ready to book a flight. I know I said I had some time off, but I was thinking more of hanging around the city.

"How about we talk about it over dinner? I know this beautiful restaurant within walking distance from the park. We can go and take a late-night stroll through the park," I said.

"I would love that. What time should I get dressed? Should we take the train or drive down and walk to the park from the restaurant," she said.

"First, relax. I will pick you up at eight forty-five. That would give me enough time to get home, shower, and change," I said.

"That's cool. I'm sorry. I am just enjoying spending time with you," Mya said.

"I like that you tell me exactly what you are feeling. You don't try and downplay your feelings," I told Mya. I loved that about her. Even when we would text, she always said what she felt.

My ex-wife used to call me emotional when I would push her to tell me how she felt about me. I remember explaining to her how I didn't feel loved or wanted, and her response was that we were married and should be the only thing I needed. With Elle, any emotional conversation we had ended in an argument.

"I wasn't always like this. I had to learn to be more open. I'm glad you appreciate it," Mya said.

"I appreciate it a lot. I don't have to guess how you're feeling and what you're thinking," I said.

"That's nice to know, even though I never know what you're thinking," Mya said.

"You want to know what I'm thinking?" I asked.

"Only if it's good," she said.

"It is. I'm thinking of how you would look in a bikini," I said.

"Come find out."

With that, we said goodbye and hung up the phone.

Toni

"So, did she ever say why she didn't answer the door last night?" Elle said.

"We barely said two words to each other all day. She's been acting really funny lately. She could barely do her damn job because she's been texting all day," I said.

Elle and I had been on the phone since I left the client's house. I knew I was feeling her head with some bullshit because J had been working hard all day. Honestly, I barely like to work, so J picks up my slack most of the time. I had been extra lazy today because of how she treated me when I came over last night. J had me fucked up.

I'm not mad that she is fucking Mya. I knew she was over there last night. I just wanted to see that shit for myself. Then she tried to throw shade like I ruined her damn night.

The problem with J is that she thinks her life is perfect, and everyone who lives differently needs to be corrected. J grew up in the suburbs of a tiny ass Alabama town and thinks she knows it all. She doesn't know shit. She thinks I don't know how she talks about me when I'm not there.

"Well, I can tell you now that she wasn't talking to me. She hasn't answered any of my calls and texts, so it must have been the other one," Elle said.

"Must be. The fact that she was just over my place talking about working things out with you, and now she's acting like this kinda pisses me off," I said.

"I'm just done with the up and down and in and out with her feelings. You were right. I deserve better. Did she seem upset at all today because I can't stop crying?" Elle said.

"All she did, all day, was smile in that damn phone. Had me doing all the work," I lied. I knew that would get to her. It wasn't a whole lie. We hadn't said one word to each other, but the hoe was smiling all day. "Mya got her feeling herself, and they both could kiss my ass."

"So, that's her name. That's the icing on the cake," she said. "I can't wait to get this drink. I need it. I'll see you in a little bit. Let me start getting dressed."

"Are you going to wear something sexy?" I asked.

"Don't play. I'm already in my feelings," she said.

"Who said I'm playing? Fuck J," I said, meaning every word. "Like I said, you deserve better."

"And you're better?" Elle asked.

"I could be," I said.

"Don't make me laugh. You forgot that I know you, and every time I see you, you're with a new chick. Like I don't know what you and J are up to at your little kickbacks," she said.

"Damn, you make me sound so bad," I said.

"No, you're not bad. You're just not ready for a woman like me," she said.

"Elle, I can show you better than I can tell you what I'm ready and well prepared for. You ain't ready for a stud like me," I said.

"Girl, I married and divorced a stud like you. I don't want another one," she said.

"I may not be what you want, but I can be exactly what you need," I said.

"I'll let you know if I ever need that, but for now, I'm good," she said.

"Noted. On that note, I'll see you in a few," I said.

"Cool. Plus, Erin is in town, and she's bringing a few people, so there will be some single ladies for you to mingle with," she said.

"Oh, so it's a party," I said, slightly upset. My plan was to chill with just Elle and me so I could get her drunk. I wanted to see the real Elle come out of her shell. Then, she might be worth my time. Now, my plans were all messed up.

"Something like that, but I'll see you then," she said and hung up. This was going to be challenging but fun, but I'm one to never run from a fight. I've been known to get what I want, even if it's in a fucked-up way.

Chapter Twelve

J

It was 8:50 p.m. when I arrived at Mya's hotel. I was five minutes late because I stopped and rolled my truck through the gas station car wash. I wanted my Rover to Sparkle in the night. I even shined my rims a little. Mya had never seen my car, so I wanted to make a good impression.

I pulled up to her hotel, and she was already waiting outside. She looked beautiful. She wore a sexy black and dark red dress with a black jacket that stopped right in the middle of her back. Her black wedge-looking shoes that were high made her legs look sexy, toned, and shiny. Her hair was pulled to the side in large curls. She looked gorgeous, and I couldn't wait to show her off.

I parked in front of her, and she squinted her eyes as if she was searching for me. I smiled, hopped out, walked around the car, and hugged her.

"You look beautiful," I said. It was true. Mya was sexy as hell.

"You clean up nice yourself," Mya said, tugging lightly on my tie. "Are we matching?"

"I guess so," I said, noticing how my red and black tie perfectly matched the color of her dress. I tipped my imaginary hat off to her and opened the door.

"Wow, this is your car," she said while climbing in. My truck was my baby. I always wanted a Range Rover, so I started making money. The moment I could afford one, I went straight to the dealership. My first car was a 2000 Toyota, a passed-down graduation gift for my mom and dad. I drove her until her engine fell out. That Toyota was my baby. She got me through some tough times. My Rover is my boo. My dream car and my success story.

"Thank you. I work hard. I figured I should play hard," I said.

Before putting the car in drive, I had to get myself a kiss. I couldn't help it. She was gorgeous, and I wanted to feel her soft lips. I leaned in, and she met me halfway. We pulled up to the restaurant, hopped out, and I quickly opened her door for Mya. I was a gentleman, especially when someone like her stepped out of my truck. She made me want to do things like open doors. I never opened Elle's door. It wasn't that she didn't deserve it; we just never went anywhere, and when we did, she opened the door before I could walk around the car. Elle was independent, but sometimes she could be too independent. I gave the parking attendant my keys and grabbed Mya's hand.

We walked hand in hand into the restaurant. I gave the waitress my name when we reached the entrance, and she immediately walked us to a table. That table was a small booth fit for two near the window, overlooking the city lights. I came here once with Elle, but we didn't sit and eat because we didn't realize it was a reservation only. We haven't been back to the restaurant since then. After a while, we stopped going out, period. I would ask her to go to dinner with me, but she would insist on cooking instead.

When the waiter sat us, I ordered a bottle of red wine and two glasses of water. When the waiter walked away, I couldn't help but stare at Mya. She caught me looking and smiled. Finally, after about ten minutes of looking over the menu, the waiter returned. I put in both orders, and she handed us our drinks.

"So, about next weekend? Is that the last week that I'm going to see you? You go back to school, right?" I said to Mya. I was curious even though I had decided to go Myrtle Beach with her. There was nothing in Atlanta for me but drama so a weekend on the beach with Mya sounded amazing.

"Yeah, it's my last week in town. That means I'm heading straight to Florida after returning from Myrtle Beach. That's why I want you to come with me. We both can use the vacation, and I think we will have a good time together," she said.

"I would love to come with you," I told her.

"Really? It will be all-expense paid," she said.

"You don't have to bribe me. I'm coming."

For the next hour or so, we talked and ate. We spoke of Mya's father and how life was before he got sick. Mya explained that life when her father got ill was hard. Her mom checked out, and she had to step in. For months, she cleaned and cooked while her mom spent time taking care of her husband, taking him back and forth to doctor visits.

After he passed, she said things got more complicated for her mom, and it was said that she wouldn't leave her room. Mya had to become an adult, planning the funeral, making sure the bills were paid on time, and caring for the house. Her mom fell into a deep depression, and although losing her dad was hard, Mya felt she had lost her mom, too.

We discussed my family back in Alabama and how I missed them dearly. I expressed my feelings for my father and explained how he hated my lifestyle.

Mya felt terrible for me because that was something she never experienced. Her family supported her decision when she came out and only wanted her to be happy.

I came out to my parents during my first year of high school, and my dad walked away as if the conversation wasn't meaningful. My mom sat quietly, and when she opened her mouth, it was to tell me that she would check on my father. I stopped talking about my sexuality and started hiding it. When I got married, I wanted my parents there to support me. Although it was a courthouse wedding, my mom was the only person who showed up.

Mya explained that it was one of the biggest things she missed about her father was that he wouldn't be able to walk her down the aisle. She said that when she was little, she would pretend to get married, holding the ceremony in her room with her dolls as guests. She said her father would always come to walk her down the imaginary aisle and hand her over to whatever doll played by the groom. If I ever got married, the chances of my father doing the same were slim to none.

We talked about Toni and her attitude these last couple of days. She made sure to tell me to watch my back when it came to Toni.

"Toni is cool," I explained.

"No, Toni is the type of person you keep at a distance. I know a person like her. I dated a person like her, and she's bad news," she said.

"You dated a person like Toni?" I asked. I couldn't believe it.

"The worst decision of my life. Just be careful," she said.

We talked about her ex and how she still had feelings. Mya explained that although she broke up with her, she still cared. She said that the girl was really nice and sweet, and she felt bad for how things turned out, but she did what she felt was right in her heart. I understood that entirely because that's how I felt about Elle. I think her for showing up when she did, but I don't feel the same way as she does, so it's best to end things now.

"I've learned not to hold on to someone if you don't see a future with them. I didn't see a future with her, so I let her go," Mya explained. I felt terrible because I didn't see a future with Elle. I also felt bad because Elle saw a future with me. My intentions were never to hurt her.

Mya was different. Being with her, I felt completely free. Her open mind and ability to see and hear me, even through texts, made me feel safe to be vulnerable with her, and I had never experienced that. For instance, I've never told anyone about my relationship with my father, and although her experience was completely different, she encouraged me to understand from his point of view. She never judged me but opened my eyes to see things differently.

When I expressed my feelings, Mya told me that a father who loves their daughter always wants her to fall in love with someone who will care for and support her, sometimes imagining them. She said that marrying a woman might not have been his image for you, but he still loves me.

"He might be upset now because it wasn't his ideal life for you, but when the right woman comes into your life, and he sees how happy, healthy, loved, and understands why you feel in love with that person, his heart will change," she said.

"We'll see. I can honestly say that I've never bought a girl like that home. They couldn't stand my ex-wife, so I wouldn't know," I said.

I confessed how Elle was tripping because she found out I was spending time with her. She listened to every word and never interrupted. When it was her turn to talk, I did the same.

It was getting late when I finally asked the waiter for the check. I paid, and we left hand in hand. I wasn't ready to end the night with her. I didn't care what we did.

"It's after ten. Do you still want to walk around the park, or are you ready to head home?" I asked her once we got outside.

"These heels are not walking heels. We can call it a night," she said. I figured as much because Piedmont Park was huge.

I gave my ticket to the parking attendant for him to grab my ride. When my truck arrived, I quickly opened the door for Mya and hopped in the driver's seat. I plugged my phone into the Aux cord, and we drove off to the sweet sounds of Trey Songz.

We passed by a bar that Elle loved to go to whenever she did go out. Out of curiosity, I slowed down to see if I could see her car. To my surprise, I spotted her car right away. Then again, it was candy red with eyelashes on the headlights. I smiled to myself. I was glad that she was getting out. I couldn't remember the last time Elle visited that bar. However, my smile faded when I noticed Toni's car parked beside hers. What were they doing out together?

"Are you ok?" Mya asked, noticing the energy shift.

"I know that's Elle's car. She's always at that bar, but I could have sworn I saw Toni's car parked next to it." I didn't want to lie to her. "No, that couldn't have been hers," I said, immediately brushing off the thought.

"I'm sure it's not," she said, trying to ease my worries. She reached her hand over and started rubbing the back of my neck. I glanced over at her, staring into the night as if she had a lot on her mind or wanted to say something but wasn't sure.

"What are you thinking about?" I said.

"Truths?" Mya said.

"Truths. You have no reason to lie to me, I said."

"I'm trying to tell myself just to go along with the flow. I'm trying not to like you," she said.

"Why?" I asked.

"Because you have baggage, and I'm not sure if you're ready to let it go, and that worries me, but I like you," she said.

"I like you too, Mya. If you are worried about Elle, I'm not going to lie. I still care for her and feel bad for her, but like you said, she's not my forever person. But I'm curious to see where this goes," I said. I wouldn't have driven past her favorite bar if I didn't care. I could have taken another route.

"That's why I like you. Your honesty is a turn-on, but I don't want to fool myself into thinking it's over between you and her," Mya said.

"You know what scares me?" I said.

"What's that?"

"This ex that you keep talking about. Is that the same ex from the park?" I ask.

"Hell no, I probably should have a restraining order on the ex from the park. I'm surprised that it went so well at the park. She's not the calmest person in the world. I haven't talked or seen her in years. I disappeared on her, but if I didn't, she would have never let me leave," she said. "The ex you're asking about, I no longer communicate with."

"That's all I need to know. I can admit that seeing Elle and Toni together bothers me, but right now, right here, is exactly where I want to be," I said.

"How can I take your mind off of it?" Mya asked.

"I know a few ways you can do that," I said.

Toni

"Damn, I think that's J," I said in Elle's ear. A small group of Elle's friends and I were sitting in the patio area at Elle's favorite restaurant, about to take another shot to pull her out of her funk.

"Yep, that's her, and she got some girl in there with her," Elle said out loud. The group turned their heads, glancing at J's all-black Range Rover.

"You okay?" Erin asked.

"Yeah, she's alright," I said.

"I was talking to Elle," Erin said. I looked at Erin like she lost her damn mind. Little did she know I was two sentences away from knocking her ass out.

"You know what, Erin? You've been throwing shots at me all night. What the fuck you got against me?" I asked.

"I don't like you," she said.

"And I don't care for your ass, but you got one more smart-ass comment."

"And what?" Erin said, interrupting my sentences. Instead of answering, I just laughed. I really wanted to pull out this pistol in my pants and slap the fuck out of that bitch, but I could hear my father's voice telling me to choose my battles. I have always had an anger problem.

"You got it, ma," I said instead.

Elle downed her shot and walked away. I followed close behind her, motioning to her friends that I had her. Elle had been drinking since we got here, and now, she was stumbling, slurring her words, and cursing J's name every time we took a damn shot. I was over it and ready to call it a night. I came up to help get her mind off J, but the alcohol worsened things. I was tired of hearing J's name, to be quite honest.

"You okay?" I said as we walked into the bathroom.

"I got to pee," she said, walking into the stale. I heard her grab a tissue from the roll and blow her nose. "I just can't believe what I just saw. I'm glad I saw it, though. I just can't accept that whatever we did have is over. I feel like it's my fault that I pushed her too fast," she said, relieving herself.

"No, it isn't your fault she has been fucking with that girl for a minute," I said, not realizing what came out of my mouth. *Damn! Fuck it.*

"Are you serious? I thought it was only a few weeks," Elle said, walking out the stale.

"Look, she may have been one of our customers on a project we did months ago. I'm only telling you this to give you closure," I said. J had already moved on. She needs to get over that shit.

"Wow," she said. Elle tried to lean on the sink but missed it completely. I caught her just in time and held her. She immediately started to cry on my shoulders.

"Look, Elle. You need to pick yourself up. J is not the only female out there. You knew how she felt, but let your feelings go there. You are beautiful, and you need to sober yourself the fuck up and move on," I said, annoyed with all that damn crying.

"I know, but it hurts," she said, lifting her head. I moved a piece of hair out of her face, kissed her temple, and helped her.

"It's time to let her go, Elle," I said.

"I'm ready to go home," she said, stumbling to the door. I was not letting her drive in this condition.

"Look, I'll take you home, okay? We can pick up your car tomorrow, but you are not driving like this," I said. Usually, I didn't care what happened to a female, but Elle was different.

"Thanks, Toni. I don't know what I would do without you," she said.

"Let me help you," I said, wrapping her arm around my shoulder. "Hold on to me."

Elle wrapped her arms around me as I helped her up. Once up, Elle kissed me on my cheek, touching my lips a little. We both jumped back and stared at each other. I knew that she was drunk and emotional, so I dismissed it. As bad as I secretly wanted Elle, this wasn't the right time.

"Come on, let's get you to the car. Just promise not to puke in my ride," I said. I paid our tab, and we walked back to the table.

"Erin, I'm about to go home. Toni is going to take me," Elle said.

"Toni is going to take you?" Erin asked.

"Man, Erin, I got her. Calm the fuck down," I said.

"Erin, please. I don't want to end your night. I just need to go home, and Toni will drive me. Don't fight me on this," Elle said.

"Just be careful," Erin said with a shrug.

Elle passed out immediately. While she rested against the window, I couldn't help but stare at her.

Those legs in that dress. She was turned to the side with her head on the window and her hands folded in her lap. Elle wasn't snoring, but I could lightly hear her breathing. She was fine as hell. I couldn't deny it. I pulled up to Elle's apartment and shook her slightly to wake up.

"Elle, we're here," I said. She blanked, reached down, and grabbed her shoes. "You need to walk you up."

"I don't think that's a good idea," she said, smiling.

"And why is that?" I said and smiled. Elle smiled back, got up, and fell right back in the seat. Unfortunately, she was too drunk, so I took the opportunity to help her to her apartment.

"Close the door, I'll Park and walk you up," I said.

She did as I said, and I parked and helped her out of the car. I held her up the entire walk to her door, grabbed her keys, and sat her on the couch.

"Sit with me for a while, please. I don't want to be alone right now," Elle said, pulling me down beside her. "I can't stop thinking about seeing J and that chick earlier."

"If I stay, no more talk about J," I said. I wrapped my arm around her and pulled her close to me.

"Just hold me," she said.

I grabbed a throw blanket and placed it over her. Within minutes, she was asleep, and I was l slowly dosing off. It was a long workday, and I didn't feel like driving back to Decatur, so I kicked off my shoes and passed out right behind her.

Chapter Thirteen

After pulling up to Mya's hotel, neither of us wanted to leave each other. Instead, we sat in the parking lot and talked about our plans for Myrtle Beach for thirty more minutes.

"You sure you don't want me to come up?" I asked, already knowing the answer. We had both agreed that tonight we wouldn't have sex, but we knew that if I went up, we would fail. I was cool because I didn't want to smother her. I wanted her to miss me a little.

"I was thinking the same thing. You sure you don't want to come up for a while?" Mya said. I groaned loudly, and she laughed, kissed me on the cheek, and exited the car.

"I'll see you soon," I said and pulled off as soon as the sliding door into the hotel closed. Mya and I had intense conversations over dinner, and we both needed to sit on the information we received. Her more than me. I know this situation with her was hard on her, and hell, it was hard on me, too. I felt like I was going through a breakup with someone I had never been in a relationship with, and Mya had been caught in the middle of the drama.

On the way home, I thought about Elle and wondered what she was doing with Toni. Everything in me wanted to call Elle and see if she was with Toni, but why would they be together? They can't stand each other. It was eating me up inside, but I decided against it again. Either way, it would start an argument. I was in a good mood and was ready to get tomorrow over, so I quickly pushed the thought of them together out of my head.

Fifteen minutes later, I pulled up to my spot, hopped out, and headed to my door. I texted Mya, told her I was home, and would call her when I got out of the shower. She texted back and said OKAY. I texted Toni and asked her if she picked up the appliances and hopped in the shower., hoping to get the answers by the morning.

After my shower, I put on some basketball shorts and a beater, grabbed a blanket, and went to the couch to find something to watch. It was a little after eleven, and I was wide awake. I called Mya once I got comfortable.

"Hey, sexy, are you in the bed yet?" I asked Mya.

"Yep, and waiting for your call," Mya said.

"I can still come over. Just say the word," I said.

"Don't tempt me. I already didn't want the night to end, especially since we didn't take a walk in the park."

"I don't think we could have only talked," I said.

"You're just bad. We have all weekend not to talk. The wedding is Saturday morning, so we have Friday, Saturday, and Sunday to have a little fun. I just hope you're not a buzz kill, and you can keep up with a girl like me," she said.

"Keep up with you? By Sunday, you're going to need another vacation fucking with me. Don't be scared because you might have met your match."

"Oh, so you think you got it like that, huh? Well, I guess we will see," Mya said.

"I suppose so. Just do me a favor and bring something sexy. I got a surprise for you," I said. I knew we couldn't keep our hands off each other, so I planned to blow Mya's mind and body in every position I could think of. I had already planned to stop by the sex store before we left. It had been years since I made a purchase.

"Are you going to tell me what you have planned?"

"I can show you better than I can tell you," I said.

"Ok, I'm going to hold you to that. Go ahead and get some sleep. I know you need to get up early, and I don't want to be the reason you're late," Mya said. I could hear her smiling through the phone.

"No, we don't want that," I said.

After that, we said good night and ended the call. I finally fell asleep after flipping through channels and watching old TV show reruns.

The following day, I woke up and got dressed. I still hadn't heard anything from Toni, so I headed straight to the garage. I pulled up to the garage. I was surprised when I saw everything packed up and ready to go. Toni must have done it before heading home last night. Which meant she expected to be late this morning.

Just as I was about to head to the customer, I got a text from Toni that she would meet me there. I texted her back and told her, cool!

Toni still wasn't there when I arrived, so I began to work. Everything was done except the appliances. Installing those was going to take little time. I planned for us to be out by lunch. It was the last job for a few weeks. As I said, I had initially planned to take a vacation back home but decided to spend the time with Mya instead.

I was more than ready to finish the day. We had been going non-stop for months, and we needed a break. We were both tired and decided to take a few weeks off before adding more clients. One thing I enjoyed about having our own company was that we could choose our schedules.

Three hours into working alone, I got a call from Toni saying she couldn't make it because she had a flat tire and was waiting for the tow truck. Her Dodge Charger apparently didn't come with spare tires. I knew she was feeding me some bullshit. She probably went out, found some new chick, and overslept. She has done this once before. But it's cool. No one was going to ruin my good mood. I was almost done anyway.

A few minutes later she called my phone.

"What's up?" I said to Toni.

"I was making sure you iight!"

"Yep!"

"Iiight!" she said. I quickly hung up the phone.

Toni

"Damn, she hung up," I said. I was still at Elle's house. I could have made it work earlier, but I didn't feel like being bothered with her. Instead, I decided to cook a little breakfast for Elle. This is a first for me. I've never cooked for anyone but myself. I expected my hoes to cook for me, but we've been vibing all morning, and I wanted to do something nice.

"You're not going to go to work?" Elle asked. We were sitting on the couch watching TV with our bellies full.

"All that's left is to hook everything up. It's not that hard. Plus, J's ass didn't help load it up yesterday," I said, grabbing our empty plate. "She will be alright."

"She will be ok," Elle said.

Elle was cool, and we learned we had much in common. We both loved old Kong Fu films and agreed that it wasn't a real flick if you didn't have to read the subtitles. She loved it because of the gruesome fighting scene, and so did I. We both feel the newer films got too soft.

After washing our plates, I walked back to the sofa and wrapped my arms around her, pulling her close and enjoying her body close to mine. She smelled so good, like coconut oil and lavender, and not like the cheap body spray or water-down perfume I was used to.

"Toni," she said, snapping out of my head.

"Yeah, baby girl?" I said.

"Did you hear me?" Elle asked, resting her head back on my shoulder.

What's up?"

"I was saying that I'm in love with your friend, and I thought she was in love with me, too. I don't understand how she could tell me she doesn't want a relationship, but not even a week later, she is riding around with the next female?" Elle said.

"Yeah, that tripped me out, too," I said.

"I'm not asking you to explain her actions because this was her choice. I'm trying to get through this, but it hurts."

"I wouldn't have the answers anyway. All I can do is be here for you," I said.

"I appreciate your company. It's better having you here than being alone," Elle said.

"I like being here," I said.

"But we both know that if she found out you were here, she would throw a fit," she said.

"Fuck J. You deserve better," I said and pulled her close to me. I need her to get this girl out of her fucking head. Elle leaned up and looked me in the face.

"What exactly are we doing? Because looking from the outside in does look wrong, Toni," Elle said.

There was a long moment of silence. I didn't know how to answer that question. What were we doing here? J is my best friend. At the same time, I will not lie and say I'm not feeling Elle. I always had.

"I don't know, Elle. I do love your company, and I also know that you love J. I can see it all in your eyes. But like you said, that was her choice, not yours. Please don't base your decisions on how you think she would react," I said.

"You're right!"

"Let's just watch TV and chill. I'm not asking anything from you but to be here as a friend," I said honestly.

My initial intentions were to piss J off and mess with J's head, but Elle didn't deserve to be played with again. If I had a girl like Elle, I would settle down.

Maybe spend all this money I've been saving and buy a house or some J ass shit like start a family.

"J can't know that you stayed the night over here," she said.

"Nah! Never! I have a question, though. If there was a chance for you and J to get back together, would you take it?" I asked. Another moment of silence.

"Yes," she said and got up. "I gotta pee."

I tried to hide my jealousy but hearing here that shit made my blood boil. When Elle returned to the couch, I grabbed her and pulled her between my legs. I wrapped my arms around her, and we finished the movie. There was no way I would let J back into her life. I'm here now!

J

Six hours later, I was finally done. I packed up the rest of the truck and headed to the garage. I wanted to be mad at Toni, but I didn't even have it in me anymore. Toni will be Toni. I was just glad that my day was over. I was ready to get home, shower, and shop for the trip. One of Elle's friends, Erin, was in town, and she hit me up earlier to see what I was getting into. We planned to meet at the mall and catch up. She said she had something to talk to me about. I was happy to meet up with her because I also needed to get some things off my chest. I also needed to go shopping for the beach. I figured I could knock two birds out with one stone.

I met Erin when Elle and I first met. She went to school with Elle before she was Erin. Erin used to be Aaron, but you could never tell. She is a beautiful half-Asian and African American trans who identified as a woman and had all the surgeries to prove it. Erin was about 5'4 with gray slanted eyes. She looks Asian, just with a darker skin tone. Her hair was jet black and hung down to the arch of her back. Elle and I hit it off immediately after meeting, and I consider her my little sister.

Toni tried to get with her, but she only dated men, and Toni was missing a few lower parts. Toni and Erin got into a nasty argument once because Erin told her she wasn't attracted to her. Toni, being who she is, thinks every girl wants her, gets instantly offended, and can't take the rejection. So now they have that "I secretly don't like you, but I can tolerate you" type of relationship. It's the fact that Toni doesn't know she's trans is the kicker.

Unfortunately, Erin never learned about her Asian heritage because her father in West Atlanta raised her. As far as she's concerned, Erin is a certified black woman who hates when someone calls her Asian. By the way she talks, you would never think otherwise. But Erin was brilliant—the top student in her class in high school and Morehouse, where she met Elle, who was attending Spelman then. That was before Aaron was Erin.

After dropping the work truck off, I hopped in my car and called Mya. She picked up on the second ring.

"Hey, you," she said. I could hear her smiling, which made me smile.

"Hey, sexy! What you up to?"

"Nothing! With my mom, we just got done getting a Mani and Pedi, then we're going to get massages," she said, sounding excited. "What are you up to?"

"Just getting off about to go home and shower, then head to the mall to pick up a few things," I said.

"I did a little shopping myself. I'm going to rent the car today," she said.

"Don't worry about the rental because we can drive my truck. I've been waiting to put her on the road," I said.

"You sure? I don't want you to put unnecessary miles on your truck. I don't mind getting a rental," she said.

"Yep, positive."

"Okay, so what are you doing after you finish shopping?" Mya asked.

"I don't know. I guess I can relax. I'm off for the next few weeks. So, I probably should enjoy it," I said.

"I can stop by on my way home. If you are back by then," she said. I immediately started smiling.

"How about you tell me when you are heading home, and I will meet you at my place," I said.

"Deal," she responded. We hung up.

Once I got home, I went straight into the shower. I told Erin I would meet her in an hour at Lennox Mall. The mall was close to me, so I had about fourty-five minutes to get dressed before heading out. I was excited about seeing her because I hadn't seen her in about three months.

I turned on my stereo and hopped in the shower. Despite the drama with Toni, I was in a good mood. Nothing could ruin this feeling. Just the thought of spending time with Mya made me smile. After the short shower, I felt brand new. Wrapped in nothing but a towel, I pulled my hair to the back in a ponytail, sprayed a little cologne, and got dressed. In forty-three minutes flat, I was out the door.

When I got to the mall, I called Erin, who told me where she had parked. I found her and parked my car beside hers. She stepped out and immediately hugged me. I picked her up off the ground and hugged her tight.

Since we first met, we have always been close. We are always talking and texting. Erin was becoming one of my best friends, and I was happy to spend time with her.

"How are you, big head?" she said as I put her down. Then, she playfully punched me on my shoulder.

"I'm good! how are you doing, smidget?" I said. Every time we see each other, we repeat the same thing. I'm her big head, and she's my smidget.

"I'm making it in this cruel world. Who are you going with to the beach? I was with Elle last night, and she mentioned nothing about going anywhere. As a matter of fact, when I asked about you, she just walked away. Somebody better tell me what's going on," she said, putting her hands on her hips.

"Elle and I are not messing around anymore. We don't even talk anymore. And for your information, I'm going to the beach with a friend," I said.

"So, are you going to tell me what happened, or is it that "I don't want to talk about it" situation?" Erin said, even making the air quotations. It forced me to laugh because she looks like a dark Asian, but you can see the black in her as soon as she talks or moves.

"It's a long story, but to make it short, she is ready for something I'm not ready for. So, we just ended it instead of forcing a relationship," I said, getting to the point.

"I figured that. It's crazy because I talked to you last week, and everything was cool. I'm sure you guys will figure this out, and if not, keep pushing forward," she told me.

"No, it's over. I don't want to even mess with your friend like that. She pulled some foul shit that made me see her true colors," I said.

"What?" she said, getting into the drama while we walked to the mall entrance.

"I got drunk with Toni and went over there the other night to work it out. When I got there, someone else was there. She would even let me go inside," she said.

"You are lying! It was probably her ex," she said.

"Yeah, that's what Toni said," I said.

"If it was, trust me, she only did that to upset you. Nothing is going on between them," she tried to explain. "She was in town visiting someone else and stopped by.

"You know, we have been arguing a lot lately. I don't matter now because I've already ended things, and I don't want to go back. I do love her. I do. I want her to be happy even if it's not with me," I said. But anyway, enough about me. How are you doing?"

"Don't change the subject. Is that the reason you are going out of town with a friend? Because you want her to be happy with someone else? Who is this friend?" Erin asked as we walked into Pac Sun.

"I've known this friend for a while. I am starting to like her, though, and I want to see where it goes. Elle and I just aren't working out. I can't force something that's not there," I said.

"Does she know about Elle?" Erin asked. "I feel like this woman popped up out of the blue. Like I said, I just talked to you, and things were fine."

"Yeah, she knows everything. I'm not trying to lie to her. Maybe she did pop out of the blue because although we've texted in the past, we've only just started hanging out," I said as I began looking through board shorts.

"And now that you're hanging out, you like her, and Elle isn't working out?" Erin said.

"You made it sound so bad."

"Because it is. I love you, but Elle is still my friend. I think she's getting the short end of the stick here.

"So, what do I do? I like the new girl a lot." I said, handing the cashier my items.

"You said you ended things? That's all you can do since you have feelings for someone else. I hope she's worth it because Elle is a great woman."

"Elle is a great woman, but I wouldn't put Elle through any of this if I thought Mya wasn't worth it," I said.

"Mya, huh?"

"Yep," I said.

"Well, now that y'all are done, you know if I have to choose between you and Elle, it would be Elle?" Erin said. "You understand that, right?"

"I'm sure."

"So, tell me about this new woman," she said as we entered the next store.

"She's pretty amazing. She's a photographer and goes to school down in Florida. She's so easy to talk to, and you know I don't like being vulnerable."

"No, you run from hard conversations," Erin said.

"Don't come for me. Seriously, though, Mya makes me feel light. The world doesn't feel so heavy when I'm around her."

"That's deep," she said.

"Right. She does have a crazy ex-girlfriend. We ran into her at the park the other day, and Mya looked terrified of her. When I asked her, she told me she was trying to get away from her," I said. It has been sitting on my chest since the run-in at the park, but I let it go once I realized how uncomfortable it made Mya. It felt good getting it off my chest.

"You think she's abusive?" Erin asked, grabbing a few more items and shoving them in my arm to try on. I held them up and walked towards the dressing room.

"I didn't ask. But Mya also told me she was talking to someone else in Florida. So, she had to be an old ex," I said.

"So, let me get this straight! She got an abusive ex who lives out of state, and she is talking to someone at school," she said.

"Well, when you put it all together, it does sound bad," I laugh.

"Yeah, you sure that's what you want? Elle has been there for you this entire time," she said as she stood outside the dressing room door.

"Honestly, even if Mya weren't in the picture, I would still leave Elle alone. Things are ending. Mya does make me happy, and I don't want to drag Elle along," I said.

"Elle is my Sorority sister, but you are my best friend. I'm glad you aren't trying to juggle two women because I would have had to beat your ass. All I'm going to say is be careful with this new girl. Ask questions," she said.

"I got you. Now, how have you been?" I said, changing the subject again.

"I've been good. I landed a good job overseas, so I'm here for a week, and then they are flying me out to Australia to work with disabled children at a children's hospital there. Why weren't you at my homecoming party the other night?" Erin asked.

"The bar on Peachtree? Damn, I was on a date. I saw Elle's car there, but she didn't tell me anything about the party. She didn't even say that you were in town. I didn't know until you texted me today," I said as we walked out of the store with more bags. "Why didn't you text me and tell me?"

"You know how Elle gets? If I sent you the invite first, I would never hear the last of it," she said. Erin was right. I knew that Elle always envied our relationship since she introduced us. She never said anything to my face, but I knew that, at times, she felt some way.

"True."

"I thought that she would invite you. I'm glad you didn't, though," Erin said.

"Why? You didn't want me to come," I said.

"No, because Elle was drunk as hell. I knew something had to be going on with you two because Toni was there too, and when I asked her where you were, I got no answer," she said.

"Toni was there? I thought I was tripping when I saw her car," I said.

"You know I don't even mess with Toni like that, but Elle invited her. I just thought it was awkward, but I left it alone. I didn't want that to ruin my good time," Erin said.

"Wow," I said.

"The last thing I saw was Toni putting her in her car and heading out. When we left, Elle's car was still out there. You know I don't like your friend, she is sneaky, and I don't trust her. I called Elle today and asked her what happened, but she never responded," she said.

I know how Toni is, but I always gave her the benefit of the doubt. I always told myself that I would be the one that she talked about the grimy shit that she has done, but never in my life would I have thought that she would pull some shit like that with me. I was boiling but trying to hide it. The thought of them together and because she didn't let me know put a bad taste in my mouth. This shit was foul.

Was that the reason she left me hanging this morning? Was that why they both had been acting funny? Was that who she was on the phone with, smiling hard the day before? This shit wasn't sitting well with me, but I pushed it aside.

"It could be nothing, J. I just wanted to let you know," she said, trying to get me to relax.

"I'm trying to let it go, but I just feel like I've been stabbed in the back," I said.

"Before you assume, ask Elle yourself. She could have dropped her off at home. She was drunk," she explained.

"Yeah, but she never picked her car back up, you said. Toni called out this morning saying she had a flat tire," I said, putting it all together. "It's not a coincidence, Erin."

Erin didn't have anything to say after that. So, we changed the conversation and finished shopping.

Chapter Fourteen

After shopping with Erin, I was more than ready to get home. But hearing about Toni and Elle had me sick to my stomach. I always knew that Toni had a thing for Elle. She would always talk shit about her being bougie, but I knew that deep down inside, she wanted her. Hell, Toni only wants what she can't have.

Within minutes, I pulled up to my apartment and grabbed all my bags. I walked in and placed them on the floor near the door. I sat on my couch and pulled out my tablet. I powered it on and kicked off my shoes. I clicked on Twitter and began reading Elle's tweets:

INTELLEGENT_ELLE:

I guess you should move on when it's all said and done.

INTELLEGENT_ELLE:

When hurt turns into anger…

INTELLEGENT_ELLE:

When you see your old chick with a new chick… Get up under the next chick.

After reading that last tweet, I immediately blocked her, which confirmed everything. I shut down my tablet, entered the kitchen, and poured myself a shot of Hennessey. I needed to get my mind right before Mya came over. After downing three shots and hopping in the shower, I was back on the couch with my feet kicked up, flipping through channels fifteen minutes later. I grabbed my phone and called Mya. She picked up on the third ring.

"Hey, love," she said.

"Hey, what are you up to?"

"Nothing just came from dinner. I was about to call you," Mya said.

"Great minds think alike. I can't wait to see you."

"I can't wait to see you either. I can be there within the next hour," she said.

"Sounds good," I said.

"Okay, I will see you then," she said. I could hear her mom trying to grab her phone in the background. They were both laughing. After a few seconds, Mya got back on the phone. "Sorry. My mom is trying to be nosey."

"So, you told her about me?" I asked.

"Maybe. Probably. Should I?" Mya said.

"That's a good question. I'm sure we will meet soon," I said.

"That's nice to hear. Yes, I did tell her about you. A little bit," she said.

"I hope all good things," I said.

"Of course, nothing negative has come up yet," I said.

"You sure? Even after our talk last night," I said.

"I'm sure. Everyone comes with baggage. It's about dealing with it before being serious with someone else," she said.

"I get it. I'll see you soon," I said.

We said goodbye and hung up. I turned to the music channel and leaned back in the chair. Within minutes, I was knocked out until the front desk called to let me know Mya was on her way up. I told them OKAY and hung up the phone.

I quickly got up off the couch and tried to straighten myself up. I turned the TV down and walked to the door. I slid on my shoes to meet Mya at the elevator. By the time I made it to the elevator, Mya was stepping out. As soon as she saw me, she smiled. I smiled back, hugged her, and grabbed her hand. We walked hand in hand to my door. As soon as we turned the corner, Tammy exited her apartment. As soon as she saw us holding hands, she smiled.

"Well, hello, neighbor. Who is this cutie?" Tammy said.

"Hey, Tammy. Tammy, this is Mya. Mya, Tammy," I said, laughing.

Tammy was never a fan of Elle. I could only imagine what she was thinking, seeing me walking with someone else. She wore her workout clothes as usual, but this time, she held a towel and water bottle in her hand.

"Hi. You're gorgeous, by the way," Tammy said to Mya, then gave me a wink.

"Thank you. You are, too. I need to head to the gym with you," Mya said.

"Anytime, baby girl. I could use a partner," Tammy said.

"Hopefully, one day we could make that happen," Mya said, speaking to Tammy but looking my way.

"Hopefully. I like her," Tammy said.

"Me too," I said and grabbed Mya's lower back, pulling her close to me. Tammy smiled. After that, she was down the hall, rushing to the elevator.

"She's pretty," Mya said.

"Yeah, don't get any ideas. Tammy's all the way straight. As straight as straight can be," I said, opening the door and letting Mya walk in front of me.

"I take it you tried?" Mya asked, getting comfortable on the couch.

"Hell no, but she's a cool person. She looks out for me for real. But Toni has," I said.

"Does Toni try to talk to everybody she meets?" Mya asked, shaking her head.

"Pretty much," I said, laughing. My bro was on a trip, but I loved her. I couldn't stand her, but I don't expect her to be anyone other than who she's shown me over the last eight years.

Mya kicked off her shoes and cuddled next to me on the couch. After flipping through all the channels and finding nothing to watch, we decided to go to the room. I gave her one of my T-shirts, and she went to the bathroom and changed. We climbed into bed and just talked and held each other.

"Can I ask you a question?" I said, after telling me about her day with her mom.

"Yeah," she said, turning over so that we could be face to face.

"What's up with you and your ex?" Why were you so scared at the park?" Mya lowered her head, and I immediately grabbed her chin and lifted it back up. "It's okay. Talk to me," I said.

"That story is far from a love story, and to be honest, it haunts me every day," she said.

"Was it that bad?" I asked. Mya took a deep breath and began.

"We were together since High School. She wasn't my first girlfriend, but she was my first serious relationship. I met her my senior year, and we dated up into my sophomore year of college. That relationship was beyond toxic, and I tried everything I could to keep the peace between us," she said.

"Did she hit you?" I interrupted. That question has been on my mind since the run-in. The way Mya tensed up had me wondering why she was so scared.

"Not at first. It wasn't until I left for college that things got bad. My first year is when it started happening. She would drive to Florida, pop up on campus, and stay for weeks, hiding in my dorm until my roommate complained. When they told her she couldn't come back on campus without a student I.D., I had to beg my parents for money so we would get a hotel room," she said.

"Did your parents know about the abuse?" I said.

"Hell no. During my sophomore year, Drea made me guilt my parents into getting us an apartment instead of me staying in the dorms. She always thought I was cheating and wanted to move to Florida with me. Unfortunately, she had no job, so I had to beg my parents again for money. I lied and told them I didn't feel comfortable in the dorm. They almost had me change schools, thinking I was in danger.

"Damn!" I said.

"Right. After we had got the apartment, things got worse. She would take my phone and car keys. She had control over my entire life. She had to take me to class and pick me up. I couldn't hang out with my friends or participate in campus activities. She couldn't come because she wasn't a student. She would be angry at me about it," she said.

"That's messed up," I said.

"When my dad got sick, we got into this big fight because I had a group project, and she thought I was trying to talk to a guy in my group. The group had to meet at the library occasionally, and one day, I lost time, and she was waiting for me. When I walked out of the library with my classmates, she was sitting on top of my car smoking a black-n-mild. When we got back to the house, she kept asking which one I was l sleeping with, but she didn't believe me, and then," she paused as tears dripped down her face and disappeared in the sheets.

"You don't have to finish. I understand," I said, placing soft kisses on her forehead.

"It was so bad that I couldn't come back to Atlanta and have my mother see me like that. I couldn't even go to class because my eyes were so swollen shut. It took about a month for my face to heal completely. It wasn't until my senior year that I could finally get away," she said.

I grabbed her face and kissed her long and slow. She relaxed. I didn't ask any more questions. After that, we both fell asleep holding each other.

Toni

After spending all day with Elle cuddled on the couch watching Kong Fu movies, I felt like Elle and I were getting somewhere. Elle even hit the blunt when I sparked up. The vibe was crazy, but I was ready to leave.

At first, she wouldn't stop talking about J's ass, but after a few blunts, she forgot all about her ass, and we spent the day with Elle lying on my lap while I played in her hair as we strolled through Netflix.

It was cool because we liked the same movies, black comedies, and Kung Fu movies.

"Can I hit that?" Elle asked as I pulled on my perfectly rolled backwoods.

"Hell no. You're not about to me over here acting like Smokey," I said.

"See, there you go, judging me again. I used to smoke all the time. I can even roll," she said.

"What? Stop playing. You can roll a backwoods?" I said, holding up my almost-gone blunt.

"Yes, I can. I lived a different life at one point," she said.

"You should tell me about that life," I said.

"Why would I do that? I didn't work so hard to put that horrible life behind me just to continue to relive it," she said.

"Yet, you're asking to smoke my shit," I said.

"I didn't mean it like that. Your life isn't horrible. I just don't get it. Why continue to act like you're a thug, but you have a degree and a business? Why not leave that life behind you?" Elle said.

"Not everyone is trying to put parts of their life behind them," I said, taking one long drag and putting it on my homemade ashtray of aluminum foil I found in Elle's kitchen drawer. Elle removed herself from my lap and sat up.

"I just don't get it. You and J are complete opposites," she said.

"That's not a bad thing," I said, moving my locs to one side and reaching for the sandwich bag on the coffee table containing my weed. "You still trying to smoke?"

"Yeah," Elle said, licking her lips and giving me that look again.

"Alright. Let's see what them rolling skills is like," I said, handing the bag to Elle.

"Okay. I got you," Elle said, grabbing the bag and pack of backwoods. I sat back and watched her as she licked the blunt to perfection. When she was done, she handed it to me for inspection. I held it in the air, rotating it slowly. Elle sat back with her arms folded, smiling at her work.

"Okay, I see you. This shit is perfect. Light it up, gangster," I said, handing the blunt back to Elle. Elle dried it like a pro, rotating it up and down under the fire. Then she put it to her lips, testing both ends before lighting one side and taking a deep pull. "Fucking sexy."

"Shut up," Elle said, then took another long puff.

"I'm about to get out of here," I said, taking the covers off so Elle could get from between my legs. She had her head resting on my chest high as hell.

We had just finished watching Ip Man, and I felt nice and ready to start my night. My homie was in town, and I was meeting up with her later.

"Okay," Elle said. Elle sat up, grabbed the blanket, and folded it. I grabbed my shoes and sat back on the couch. "This can't happen again."

I immediately got annoyed but quickly brushed it off. I grabbed Elle and sat her down next to me. I placed my hand on her thigh.

"Elle, nothing happened. We just watched movies," I said.

"I know, but this is still wrong. I did enjoy your company, though. It's crazy how we have so much in common," Elle said.

"I know. I enjoyed myself too. I even cooked for you, and I never do anything like that," I said. I knew I shouldn't, but my feelings were emerging. Or the feelings that I always had were starting to resurface.

"I didn't even know you could cook," she said. I grabbed my hat and stood up. J didn't know what she had. If Elle were my girl, I would cater to her like the queen is. I needed to get out of there before I started telling her my true feelings.

"There's a lot of things you don't know about me. Maybe you should try to get to know me one day," I said.

"Is that right? What else do I not know about you?" Elle said, licking her lips and fixing her messy bun.

"Wouldn't you like to know? I'm about to get out of here. I'll call you later," I said. I pulled her off the couch to me. She wrapped her hands around my neck and hugged me tightly. I wrapped my arms around her waist and buried my face in her neck. We held on for a few more seconds before separating.

"Okay," she said and led me to the front door. I kissed her on her forehead and left. I needed to get home and shower. Elle threw me off with all that cuddling and shit. It felt nice, though.

Before getting in the car, I texted Shonda and asked if I could come over later. After dry humping with Elle, I was horny and needed to relieve some stress. At least, that is what cuddling was to me... dry humping.

Shonda texted back immediately and said OKAY. I got in my car, put it in drive, and proceeded to my house to get cleaned up. I have not seen my bro since she moved back to Atlanta. She's been back for a while, but I've been so busy we haven't had a chance to catch up. I needed to chill and hang out. I had fun with Elle and her friends, but that wasn't my crowd, and I felt like I was babysitting Elle all night. I couldn't wait to turn up and get drunk. It's always a party when my bro comes into town.

J

The following day, we woke up still in each other arms. I rolled over and placed soft kisses on Mya's forehead. She moaned softly and moved closer to me.

"Good morning," she said, buried in my chest.

"Good morning," I said, kissing her as I held her tighter. She kissed me on the lips and rolled over.

"What time is it?" Mya asked. She reached over, grabbing her phone off the charger. I rolled over and went for my own. I clicked the button to unlock the screen.

"A little after nine," I said. I pulled down the notification bar to see that I had three text messages, all from Elle. I immediately got annoyed but pushed it out of my head as I sat my phone down and turned my attention to Mya, who had begun getting dressed.

Even though the conversations about her ex got a little emotional last night, I still enjoyed Mya's company. I hate comparing her to Elle, but I get a different vibe from Mya. Even talking to her is easy, and I love that she opens up to me without me having to ask question after question to get an understanding. With Elle, our conversation always ended with saying that we didn't want to discuss it or agree to disagree. None of that works if there is no understanding. With Elle, there was no intimacy or vulnerability. Those two things are so important when connecting with someone. I think deep down inside, Elle knows this too.

"I have to meet my mother in half an hour. I forgot to set my alarm. She already called me twice," she said.

"Okay, that's cool," I said. I picked back up my phone and clicked on Elle's message.

Elle: You need to come and get your stuff.

Elle: Um, hello!

Elle: You must be with that bitch! You have until today to pick up your things, or they're going in the trash.

Me: OMG, I'll be there in an hour. Just have my shit ready, man.

I sent the text and put my phone on the table, grabbing my forehand in frustration. Elle tried to ruin my day, but I wouldn't let her. Not today.

"Are you okay?" Mya asked. She was done getting dressed and was walking into the bathroom to brush her teeth.

"No, I have to go get my things from Elle's. She's talking about throwing my stuff out. I don't even want to go over and hear her shit, but I have work clothes and tools over there, and I don't need her messing with any of my things. The clothes I could care less about, but I need my tools," I said, grabbing my shorts. We both continued to dress in silence. Within fifteen minutes, we were heading to our cars.

"What's on your mind?" I asked Mya on the elevator.

"I feel like my presence is causing you problems and making you make big decisions," she said.

"I'm not going to lie. The whole week has been crazy," I said. Before I could finish, the elevator stopped, and someone got on. Once we got to the parking garage, we got out, and I followed Mya to her car. She unlocked the door, and I opened it for her.

"You didn't cause any of this. Elle and I were done way before you entered the picture. I've just been too busy to focus on her," I said.

"What's going to happen when we come back and I leave for school?" she asked, looking at her looking at me with worried eyes.

I could see her soul through the circle of her pupils. Mya had the same fear of falling in love as I did, and I didn't have an answer. All I knew was Elle; my relationship was dead, and I was falling for Mya. Hard.

"I don't know. All I know is that I like you, and I hope you don't dodge my calls when you get back to Florida," I said. I leaned inside the car and kissed Mya on the cheek.

"I like you too. No, I'm not going to dodge your calls. I'm just huge on transparency. I need to know where we are on the same page," she said.

"Do I have to worry about the girl in Florida once you go back?"

"Who? I blocked her the day after the park. I'm yours if you want me, J. But you must take care of that baggage before that door could even be opened," she said.

"Noted," I said.

With that, she pulled off. I quickly walked to my car. I needed to hurry up and get this shit with Elle over. I knew she wouldn't make this easy, but I had time today.

I pulled up to Elle's in record time and parked in the first available space. Within minutes, I was knocking on her door. She opened the door in short, silky pajama shorts and a white spaghetti-strap shirt that stopped above her belly button.

Fuck! She looked good as hell. I tried to walk past Elle, but she pulled me close, trying to kiss my neck. I pushed her away and went to retrieve my things.

"So, that's where we are now? You're pushing me away?" she said, walking behind me.

"I didn't come here for that. Didn't you ask me to get my things before you throw them out?" I asked Elle.

"You know I wouldn't throw them out. I didn't know how else to get you over here," she said, grabbing me from the back and placing her arms around my waste. I wiggled out of her grip.

"Stop. I'm not doing this with you. I just want to get my things," I said.

"Doing what?" Elle said and stood before me, pressing her chest to mine. "We fight. We make up and fight again. It's what we do."

"That's the thing. I'm done doing all of that," I said.

I didn't want to play the games anymore with Elle. I wanted an adult conversation, but I knew what she was on when she opened the door. She was looking sexy as hell, and she knew I loved her in those pajama shorts. Images of her sitting on the sofa reading with her legs crossed and her glasses hanging off her face flashed in my head. Two months ago, I would have ripped that shit off her and fuck all that attitude right up out of her. She would cry when we were done and fall asleep on my chest.

"Why because of Mya?" Elle asked. Hearing Mya's name come out of Elle's mouth upset me. I never said her name or even mentioned her around Elle. Now I know what the topic of discussion was the other night.

"Don't say her name, Elle. Just let me get my things and get out of your way," I said. I moved Elle to the side and began grabbing my tools.

"So, it's true. You're leaving this for her?" Elle asked. I stopped and turned to face her. I grabbed her hands and led her to the sofa.

"Elle, sit down," I said. She sat down slowly.

Looking at her holding back tears, I felt sorry for Elle. But I quickly realized it's what we have done for the last six or so months. Like she said, we would fight and make up and make up to fight again. I've always had one foot out the door, but she pulls me back when I get too close to the exit.

"Stop acting like we were perfect, Elle. Yes, the beginning was fun, but all we've been doing lately is arguing. We don't even talk and text during the day or flirt anymore. Elle, can you honestly say that you're happy with me?" I said.

"You're not even going to give us a try. All relationships have their moments. I've been here fighting for us, but I can't be the only one fighting," Elle said as the tears fell. I got up off the couch and gathered my things. I knew where the conversation was going.

"You've been fighting for us? Elle, I saw you and Toni at the bar the other night. What was up with that? Did you leave with her?" I said.

"I was drunk. Toni dropped me back here and left," Elle said, shifting in her seat, trying to cover herself up with a throw pillow.

"Really?" I said with a laugh. I grabbed my tool bag with one hand and the small bag of clothes with the other. Elle followed me to the door.

"It's not like you care any fucking way. You saw us at the bar, but we saw you with that bitch, too. So don't worry about what the fuck I do. I'm no longer your concern," she said.

"You expect me to believe that you and her just hung out? Toni don't just hang out with anybody. But you're right. I don't care what you do, and you're not my concern," I said. I couldn't lie and say that the thought of Elle and Toni together didn't upset me. It hurt because I knew Toni had a thing for Elle. I didn't believe she would act on it. I held back tears and placed all my belongings in a trash bag. I wasn't even mad at Elle. I felt betrayed more by Toni. If Elle allowed herself to get trapped in Toni's game, that was on her.

"You really are leaving?" Elle asked.

"Yes," I said, grabbing the rest of my things and walking out. I heard Elle scream, "fuck you," as I exited the door. She slammed the door behind me, and I continued to the elevator with my trash bag filled with clothes and tools.

I was beyond hurt that Elle would lie to me. There was no way Toni dropped her off and went home. Why didn't she show up to work the following day if Toni was sober enough to drive Elle to her condo and go home? I didn't believe that flat tire bullshit because Toni never went without a car. If they had to tow it, as she said, she would have gotten a rental before the car reached the mechanic. Nothing she said was adding up. I was happy we weren't taking on any jobs for a few weeks. I didn't know how I could face Toni. I needed to get out of Atlanta.

After setting everything in my truck, I called Erin and briefly told her what transpired, and she immediately gave me her address. I pulled up to her place in less than ten minutes. Erin's family owned a nice brownstone home downtown. Erin had been staying there on and off for as long as I've known her. When she isn't in town it's used as an Airbnb.

"Girl, okay. Do you really think Toni spent the night?" Erin asked as soon as I sat on the sofa.

"I know Toni spent the night."

"You think they slept together?" Erin asked.

"Nah, she wouldn't have called me there ready for sex. It was never about my things. She was trying to sleep with me. I know Toni always liked Elle. I'm not stupid. I'm sure Toni would have been the perfect gentleman if she stayed the night."

"That's even scarier," Erin said. "You want a drink? You need a drink."

"Please. I can't believe Elle would even fall for it. Toni, I expect that, but not from Elle," I said.

"Yeah, it's tripping me out too. I can't stand Toni. I was taken aback when she showed up at the restaurant with Toni and not you," she said, handing me a beer.

"Imagine how I felt seeing both of their cars at that bar," I said.

"So, about this girl, you really like her?" Erin asked as we sat down.

"I do. I want to see where this goes," I admitted to Erin.

"I know Elle. She isn't having it, huh?" she said.

"She has no choice, and I don't want to waste any more of her time," I said.

"So, what makes this new girl so special?" Erin asked.

"Everything from the way she makes me feel to our communication and even the sex," I said with a huge grin.

"Throw it all out there," she said.

"Well, you asked. For real, Elle isn't the easiest person to be with. Her insecurities alone are too much. I can't do anything or take her anywhere because we are arguing or she's rude because someone spoke to me. I can't deal with that," I said.

"Elle has been through a lot, from cheating to abusive relationships and everything else. I knew she had some issues, but I didn't realize how deep her insecurities ran," she said.

"It's not my job to fix her. Elle is damn near ten years older than me, but sometimes I feel like she's either trying to parent me or acting as if she needs to be parented," I said.

"I can see that. I'm sorry, J," she said.

"It's cool. I don't know why everyone is acting like this is something new. Elle and I relationship were dead before Mya got here. Mya just gave me motivation to walk away," I said.

"I hear you. I talk to y'all all the time, and things never seem like they were "dead' as you put it," Erin said.

"We never said they were good either," I said.

"No, you haven't," Erin said.

I spent the rest of the day drinking with Erin. Mya texted me earlier and said she would stay with her mom and would call me before bed. I was cool with that because Erin had me already drunk, playing foosball in her game room.

Chapter Fifteen

The following day, my phone ringing woke me from a deep slumber. I was laid across my bed, fully dressed. The moment I rolled over, the world spun, and I felt myself about to vomit. I closed my eyes and felt for my phone.

"Hey, good morning," Mya said through the speaker.

"Hey love, what are you doing up so early?" I said.

"It's after ten."

I tapped my phone. It was 10:34 a.m., and I couldn't remember what happened last night.

"Damn, it is?" I said, rolling out the bed.

"You don't have to get up. I was wondering if I would see you today. I know we leave in the morning, but I wouldn't mind staying with you tonight," she said. I rolled out the bed and stumbled to the bathroom.

"Hold on," I put my phone down, quickly hugging the toilet and throwing up everything I must have drunk the night before.

"Are you okay?" Mya said through the speaker.

"I'll call you back," I said. I hung up the phone and resumed puking out a thick orange substance. After about five minutes of vomiting, I pulled myself up to the sink. My phone vibrated on the floor.

"Hey, babe! I'm okay," I said.

"Hey, it's Erin. But I'm glad you're okay," Erin said.

"Oh dang, my bad. Erin, what happened last night?" I asked her. I turned off the bathroom lights and climbed back into bed, pulling the covers over my head.

"That was you, taking shots with them white boys. I told you to slow down. I had to drive you home and catch an Uber back," Erin said. Pieces of the night flashed in my head. The last thing I remembered was leaving Erin's place and walking to the bar down the street from her house.

"Damn, thanks E. I woke up throwing up everything. I don't remember anything, but I know I needed that. I'm sorry you had to catch an Uber," I said

"Yeah, I figured I'd get you home since you kept asking for Mya's ass," she said.

"Mya! Oh shit! Let me call you back," I said. I hung up the phone and immediately called Mya. She picked up on the first ring.

"Are you okay?" Mya asked.

"Yeah. I'm good. I'm a little hungover. What were you saying?" I said.

"I'm picking up the rental today. My mom is going to get my car serviced while we are gone. I thought I could stay with you tonight," she said.

"I thought we talked about this. I told you we could take my truck," I said.

"And I told you I don't want to put unnecessary miles on your car," she said.

"And I'm telling you that I don't mind. As a matter of fact, I want to. Just go with it, Mya," I said.

"Oh, is this our first argument? This is sexy!" Mya said.

"Stop being silly," I laughed. "I'm serious."

Well, okay. Are you feeling okay? Did you have a long night?" Mya said.

"I'm a little hungover, but I'm good," I said.

"What did you get into? Did you get your things from your ex?" Mya asked.

"She's not my ex, and yes. Would you believe she opened the door half-naked and trying to sleep with me?" I said.

"I could see that," Mya said, laughing.

"Yeah, it was crazy. When I finally got out of there after pushing her off me, I hung out with my friend. We had some drinks and played foosball," I said.

"Well, at least your day turned around," she said.

"It did. What did you and your mom get into?" I asked.

"Shopping. That's about it. We had breakfast and lunch while we were out. By the time we got home, I passed out," she said.

"That sounds like fun. Did you miss me?" I asked.

"I did. I tried not to worry about the whole getting your things situation, but I had hoped that everything went smooth," she said.

"As smooth as it could have, but I have my things, and it's clear that the non-relationship is over," I said.

"Noted. Are you going to be able to pick me up since you're adamant about driving your vehicle?" Mya said.

"Why wouldn't I be able?" I asked.

"I don't know. You're sounding a little hungover over there," she said.

"You must not know about me. All I need is some aspirin and a bottle of water. I'll be there at five," I said.

"Okay, at least try and get some rest," she said.

"Fine. I'll get some rest. I'll call you later," I said.

"Yes. I can't wait to see you."

"Me either," I said.

After hanging up with Mya, I set my alarm for noon and fell asleep. When I awakened, I was still a little hungover, but I shook it off and continued my day like always. My college days made this hangover feel like a mild headache. I needed a few more things done, like an oil change, so I quickly got dressed and headed out.

After doing all my running around, it was after seven when I was finally on my way to pick up Mya. It hit me: the last time I saw her mother, we were remodeling her kitchen. I began to get nervous because I didn't know how she would feel about a construction worker dating her daughter. The night was going to be interesting. So, I decided to call Mya and see what was up. As always, she picked right up.

"Hey, you," she said after the third ring. I smiled. Even in school, she always texted right back or picked up. I loved her consistency.

"Hey, I was wondering. The last time I saw your mother, I worked in her kitchen. How do you think she would feel about me picking you up? Or dating?" I said, sliding in that last part. I wondered about our title, but I would be okay moving forward together.

"I knew you were going to ask me that. My mom doesn't know who is going to pick me up. She only knows it's someone I really like and have been hanging with since I've been here."

"But she doesn't know it's the same person who remodeled her kitchen?" I asked.

"Not at all. It will be a surprise. When hen you guys were here, she told me you were cute. So that's a good sign," she said.

"Thank you, I guess," I said, laughing.

"I know you're not scared of my mother. She is harmless. She hated my ex because she wasn't doing anything with her life. You have your own company, and you are kind to me. You're already winning. I'm sure that if it were her choice, you would be the person she would choose for me, so don't worry. She's going to be happy," she told me.

"The pressure," I said.

"Seriously, I tell her about you all the time. The only reason I didn't tell her who you were was that I wasn't sure if it was even necessary at the time," she said.

"So, will you tell her before I get there?" I asked her.

"No, the surprise would be epic. Don't worry. My mom has always been supportive of my lifestyle. She's going to love you," she said.

As nervous as I was, I let it go. I trusted her. But I've always been weird around parents. My ex-wife's family hated me because she married a woman. They never attended our wedding or were interested in getting to us as a married couple. I've gotten doors slammed in my face and told I wasn't allowed in her parent's home. It's safe to say that I preferred not to meet her mom, but I trusted Mya.

"Ok, well, I'll be there in twenty minutes," I said.

"Alright, I'm all packed and waiting. Hurry up and get here. I hope you haven't eaten because my mother is feeding us," Mya said and hung up quickly.

I liked how she threw that in and then hung up the phone. She was slick, but it was cute. I turned up my radio and let Drake's emotional ass speak the truth in my ears while I mentally prepared myself for this dinner. I couldn't believe how things could change so quickly. I was happy for once in a long time. There was something about Mya that drew me to her from day one.

When I met Mya, my feelings for Elle were dying. Maybe that's why I couldn't be the person Elle wanted me to be. On the other hand, Mya is everything Elle isn't and everything I was looking for in a woman and a friend. I knew Elle was just a distraction from my feelings for my ex-wife. Her love healed that pain. I hated myself for putting her through the last week or so. But I can't change the fact that I fell for Mya. I finally admitted that to myself.

Twenty minutes later, I arrived at the familiar house, but it was for a different reason this time. I knocked on the door, and immediately, her mother opened the door with Mya standing behind her.

"So, this is the mystery lady? She said to Mya, then quickly looked at me. "How are you?"

"I'm fine, and how are you?" I said with a smile. Mya opened the door wider so that I could see her standing behind her mom. Her mother stepped to the side and put her hand on her hip.

Mya's mom stood about 5'8 with a nice figure. She looked like she worked out and always kept her body in shape, even after having her only child. She wore a curly fro that matched perfectly with her honey-colored eyes. She had slight wrinkles around her mouth but looked no more than forty and could pass as Mya's sister any day. She was just as beautiful as Mya. I never noticed how much she looked like her mom, and then again, I was more focused on finishing the job when we first met.

"I'm making it. You look familiar," Mya's mom said, trying to figure me out.

"Mom, let her in the house," Mya said. Her mother stepped to the side, and I walked in. Mya hugged me, and we followed her mother into the kitchen. The kitchen looked beautiful, and she decorated it well. I was amazed. The table was set with three plates and untouched food.

"Have a seat. What's your name? Mya didn't even introduce us," she said, eyeing her daughter.

"That's because you were all in her face, mother," Mya said while laughing.

"My name is Janice. Your home is beautiful, and your kitchen came out nice," I said, admiring the familiar place.

"Mom, you know her. She's the one that did your kitchen," Mya finally said.

"Oh my gosh, I knew you looked familiar. How are you, Honey? I love my new kitchen, and thank you for your work. I referred a few of my neighbors to your company," she said, smiling.

"I'm okay. Your kitchen did turn out nice."

"Thank you, Honey. So, did you meet the day you were here or," she said.

"Mom!"

"I'm just saying. This can't be a coincidence," Mrs. Autumn said.

"Should you tell her, or should I?" I asked, referring to Mya running up and sliding her number in my hand. Mya shot me an evil glare.

"Well, since you must know, Mother," Mya said, turning her attention to her mom. "I shot my shot and gave her my number before she left that day."

"Mya!'

"What, Ma? She's fine as hell with a career," Mya said, pointing in my direction. I blushed. Mya's mom got up from the table.

"I need a drink. Y'all can fix your food," Mrs. Autumn said and walked out, but not before I saw the wink, she gave Mya. Mya looked at me and smiled.

"I think my mom likes you," Mya said, smiling from ear to ear.

"Yeah, I saw the wink she gave you. What can I say? I'm a mom magnet," I said, popping my collar. She laughed and flicked me off. Her mother came back in with a bottle of wine and three glasses. We sat down and blessed the food. Mrs. Autumn made a tuna casserole, one of my favorite meals.

During dinner, Mya's mom drilled me, asking questions about my family and what I wanted to do in life. I answered them honestly. It wasn't like she was being rude, but she wanted to learn about me and my life. Overall, I enjoyed the conversation.

Two hours later, I was putting Mya's bags in my truck, and she was hugging her mother goodbye. I saw them talking, but I couldn't make out what they were saying, so I walked over. Not to be nosey, but to say goodbye. It was getting late, and we had an early morning.

"So, Janice, please drive safe, don't speed, and care for my daughter. Thank you for staying for dinner," she said while reaching for a hug.

"Thank you, Ms. Autumn, and she's in good hands. Again, thanks for your hospitality," I hugged Mrs. Autumn, turned to Mya, and told her I'd be in the car and to take her time. She said OKAY, and I left them alone with their conversation.

A few minutes later, Mya got in the car, reached over, and kissed my lips softly.

"Thank you for coming," she said.

"You're welcome."

I put my car in drive and pulled off. I was ready to get home and get in the shower. I had been running around all day and wanted to rest before we hit the road in the morning. I turned the music up and hopped on the highway. A few minutes later, Mya reached over, turned the radio down, and cleared her throat.

"My mom said she likes you. I told her that we were just friends, and she just looked at me like I was crazy. I don't know if she likes you because you did such a good job in her kitchen or because you're so polite and sweet," she said, adjusting in her seat. I looked over at her and smiled.

"It's because of my swag," I said jokingly. "I told you your mom was feeling me, but what can I say? I'm a charmer."

"Charmer? Yeah, right, don't get cocky because you're not all that," she said playfully.

"Oh, I'm not? You are feeling me, too," I said.

"I'm not feeling you yet. But you can't wait for that, can you?" Mya said, licking her lips. I couldn't deny Mya's sex appeal, which drove me crazy. I pulled my truck over on the highway and removed my seat belt.

"What are you doing?" she asked as I turned the lights off and reached over to her side.

"Feeling you," I said. I licked my lips, slowly grabbed Mya's face, and kissed her deeply. Mya moaned as I grabbed the back of her neck with one hand and slid my hand between her legs with the other. I gripped her inner thigh and sucked her bottom lip.

I began to massage the inside of her thigh and ran my hand up her shorts. I moved her panties to the side and touched her sweet spot. She arched her back and opened her legs, inviting me inside. She gripped my wrist and pushed my hand deep inside of her. With two fingers, I slowly moved them in a "come here" motion. I could feel Mya's pussy getting wet, which turned me on even more.

"Pull these down," I said, still inside of her. She did as she was told while moving her hips to the rhythm of my fingers, not missing a beat.

I could hear the cars speeding past in between her moans. The music was still playing low in the background. Song after song, I worked my fingers inside her. She leaned against the car door, placing one on the dashboard and the other between the driver and passage seat, giving me more access to her sweet spot.

I stuck another finger inside her, causing her to arch her back more. The deeper I went inside of her, the louder she moaned. I curved my finger a little and, with my free hand, rubbed her clit. She gripped my wrist and started to move her hips wildly fucking my fingers. Her breathing increased, so I picked up speed.

"Oh my god, baby. Don't stop. I love it," she said.

I let her take control of my hand as she moved it in and out of her treasure, rotating her hips. Within seconds, I felt her body jerk and become still. Her mouth opened wide, her eyes closed, and her head tilted back slightly to the left. I felt her muscles pulsating as she climaxed. I could feel the wetness growing on my fingers. She held my hand deep inside her as I moved my fingers around in a circular motion.

When her breathing slowed, I slid my hand out of her and put one finger in my mouth. She tasted so sweet, as sweet as my favorite candy. She grabbed my hand and licked the other finger clean. I smiled, put the car in drive, and got back on the highway.

"What was that about?" she asked. I laughed.

"I told you that you're feeling me. You better watch out before you fall in love," I said. That was the first time I ever did something that wild. I was excited and horny, but I was fulfilling one of my fantasies, and Mya didn't even know it.

"Love? What's that?" she said, looking at me sideways.

"And I'm the cocky one?" I said.

"I'm glad you enjoyed that because that's all you're going to get this weekend," she said.

"Yeah, right. Just wait till we get back to my spot," I said, turning up the music. The rest of the way, we drove silently, listening to Trey Songz while she played in my hair. I could feel her glancing at me randomly; all I could do was smile. Something about her makes all the drama in my life disappear. I couldn't help but wonder if she was thinking the same thing as me. All I knew was that I needed this break, and I was happy it would be with her.

After stopping by Walmart and picking up a few snacks for the road and a scary movie for tonight, we finally pulled up to my place. We were both overly excited about the trip and knew we would be up all night with anticipation, even though we both agreed that we needed a good sleep.

I parked my truck, got out, walked around, and opened her door while she got her things and a couple of bags together. I grabbed the bags and helped her out of the car. We walked hand in hand up to my apartment.

After unlocking the door, she walked in, grabbed the bags from my hand, and took them to the kitchen. I couldn't help but look at her ass when she walked by me. I was lusting hard for her but had to get it together. I took off my shoes and placed them neatly at the door. Working in my field, I was used to taking off my shoes at the door to avoid tracking all kinds of paint and dirt on my carpet.

As soon as I pulled off my shirt, there was a knock on the door. In just a beater, I walked out of the room to look for Mya. She was in the kitchen still unpacking the snacks, putting them in a tote bag and cooler. She looked at me and then pointed at the door.

"Are you going to get that?" Mya asked.

"I have no idea who it could be," I said, walking towards the entrance.

Chapter Sixteen

I looked out the peephole, but before she could knock again, I swung the door open with a look that said, "What the fuck are you doing here?"

"Can I come in?" Elle said with sad eyes. I looked back at Mya, who was peeking around the corner with a Capri Sun in her hand. I smiled and motioned for Mya to give us a minute. Mya nodded her head and walked into the room.

"Yeah," I said, returning my attention to Elle as Mya closed the door loud enough for us both to hear.

"You have company?" Elle asked.

"Something like that," I said, stepping to the side and allowing Elle to enter. Elle walked in, looking around my apartment. I closed the door behind her.

"It took everything in me to come up here and apologize about the other night," she said. Mya's bags were still by the door, and you could see the cooler and snack boxes on the counter. "You are going on a trip?"

"Yeah, I'm going to the beach for the weekend. I need to get away and clear my head," I said with a smile. The thought of spending the weekend away from Atlanta and with Mya had me geeked.

The TV cut on in my bedroom, and Elle immediately turned toward the sound. She looked at me, and I could see the anger building up in her eyes. Then, she stormed off toward the bedroom.

"Where the fuck are you going, Elle?" I said. I followed her toward the sound. She had a crazy look in her eyes that made me nervous. She put her hand on the bedroom doorknob and slung the door open, storming into the room. Mya stood on the side of my bed with her jeans on and no shirt. She jumped, trying to cover herself quickly. Embarrassed for her, I walked in front of Elle, blocking her view of half-naked Mya.

"Get the fuck out, Elle. Don't come over here starting shit," I said, grabbing her arm.

"Don't fucking touch me," she said and snatched it away. She turned to walk out, and when she reached the front door, she turned to face me. She had a fire in her eyes of nothing but hate. I matched her evil glare with one of my own. Everything Erin told me popped into my head.

"You ain't shit," Elle said with hate.

"You ain't no better. You're nothing but a hoe anyway," I stated with the same evil glare.

"I'm a hoe? Speaking of the bitch that's ready to jump ship a few days after she got out of a relationship. You're the hoe. I'm just trying to catch up with you," she said

"That's your problem. We were never in a relationship," I said.

"I guess that is my problem because you never told me otherwise until she," Elle said, pointing towards the bedroom. "Got here."

"You know what they say about assumption."

"Fuck you, and I really hope you have fun. I can't believe I ever trusted your ass. You couldn't wait to end things. You ain't shit," Elle said, stepping up to my face. I looked her up and down, daring her to do anything crazy. I've never put my hands on a female, but I would beat a bitch ass. Instead of challenging the thought, she turned and walked away.

"I'm sure you would be alright between your ex and Tony. You're in good hands. Get the fuck out of my life, Elle."

"FUCK YOU, J," Elle said and stormed out. I slammed the door as soon as her feet crossed the threshold. *Fucking tramp.*

I turned back to Mya, who was fully dressed and enjoying the view from my door. She playfully snapped her fingers like a black woman and returned to the room. I didn't even know why it bothered me so much. I didn't want Elle. I knew that for a fact. It was the Toni and Elle thing that was making my skin crawl.

"I'm going to take a shower," Mya said.

Fifteen minutes later, Mya walked out of the shower in nothing but a towel. I sat there watching her lotion herself. I moved to the side of the bed and grabbed the lotion bottle. She looked at me and smiled. I put lotion on my hand and rubbed and massaged her whole body. She let out light moans as I rubbed lotion on her thighs. I ensured that when I made it to the inner thigh, my thumb rubbed her clit slightly. When I was done with her entire body, I climbed on top of her and kissed her on her neck. She tilted her head back and wrapped her hands around my waist, pulling me close.

"I don't want this to end," she whispered. I kissed her eagerly as my hips started to grind on her pelvis. I was crazy about this girl and hadn't even realized it yet. I just knew that I wanted her in my life.

"Neither do I," I said.

After about twenty minutes of grinding and kissing each other, she told me to stop and reminded me that it was already late and that we had to get up at five in the morning. I agreed and climbed behind her. I wrapped my arms around her and pulled her close to me. She kissed the back of my hand and rested her head under my chin. My little spoon.

"So, that was Elle?" Mya said.

"Yeah, that was Elle. I'm sorry about that," I said.

"Here we go, apologizing again," Mya laughed.

Mya was right. First, I thought about the park and Toni, and now Elle. The last few days, all we've been doing is apologizing.

"Yeah, but I wouldn't change anything. I love being with you," I told Mya.

"I love being with you," she said, pulling me closer.

We slowly fell into a peaceful sleep, holding each other close. My worries about my relationship with Elle went out the window, and my friendship with Toni followed. Finally, I felt free of my fears, even though it was only temporary. I knew that when we returned, I would have to face these problems alone and that Mya would be gone. But for now, I was going to enjoy my vacation.

Toni

I was sitting in my game room playing Call of Duty with a blunt in my mouth when I heard someone banging on my door. I rolled my eyes because I thought I met this shorty at McDonald's drive-thru. I had just got through tearing that ass up not even twenty minutes ago, and she was back already. I hate needy hoes, but she was fine as hell.

She was this light-skinned cutie with hazel eyes and a fat ass. She told me she was straight, but after a few weeks of stopping there to order breakfast, I finally convinced her to give me her number. I played the friend for a while until her boyfriend acted up and all it took was a few shots and a blunt, and she was bouncing on my strap. When she texted, me saying she wanted to see me, I couldn't help myself. I told her how to get here, and it didn't take more than two hours to fuck her right and send her home.

I got up from the beanbag, pulled on the blunt again, and sat it in the ashtray. I had basketball shorts and no shirt on, so I grabbed my beater from my room and headed to the door. I looked through the peephole and saw Elle standing there, looking eager and sad simultaneously. I rolled my eyes in the back of my head, hoping she didn't ruin my high with that tragic and emotional shit. I opened the door, still sliding on my beater.

She pushed the door open and attacked me into the wall. My beater was half on when she grabbed it and took it back off. She ran her hands down my toned stomach and around my back, looking me dead in the eyes.

I was confused and shocked. I didn't know what to do, and my facial expression matched how I felt. I was about to ask Elle what had gotten into her when she put her finger up to my lips and kissed me softly and deeply. I ignored the tears I felt when I grabbed her face and kissed her back.

I picked her up and carried her into my bedroom even though I had another female in there not even an hour before, and I hadn't changed the sheets. I laid her down on my bed.

"Are we doing this, Elle?" I asked her as my hands trailed her body, making their way between her legs. She was moaning and enjoying the feeling.

"Fuck me, Toni," she said, grabbing my dreads and pulling me closer to her. So, I did what I was told and fucked her in every position I could think of for the rest of the night without asking any more questions.

I woke up the following day with Elle next to me, naked. Immediately, I felt guilty. J was my best friend, and I would kill another person for her, but I was tired of her thinking she was better than me. I could pull a bitch like Elle, and I did. I felt like a king with Elle next to me.

I uncovered Elle's face and kissed her on the cheek. She blinked slowly and opened her eyes. Even though she smiled, I could see the shame. I took her chin and kissed her on the forehead, reassuring her that everything was ok. I got up, grabbed the black robe that I got specially made with the word "King" on the back in diamond, and walked into the kitchen. I decided to cook breakfast while she got her thoughts together.

I didn't feel like talking about the shit or what led her to my apartment. I already knew that it had something to do with J. I was just glad that she did. The entire time I was cooking, she stayed in bed. I knew she probably regretted it or felt guilty. I walked into the room and sat her plate on the nightstand. She was sitting on the bed, half-dressed, curled up in a ball.

"What the hell happened, Toni?" Elle asked as soon as I sat down.

"We had sex," I said. I grabbed my fork and started eating.

"This isn't bothering you?" she asked, grabbing her shirt and tossing it over her head.

"No," I said, taking another bite of my food. "We are both grown and single."

Elle thought the same thing because she grabbed my plate, climbed over me, and kissed my neck.

"I'm sorry. I didn't mean to ruin the moment. I have a lot on my mind," Elle said.

"Clearly! Elle, why did you come over here?" I asked. For a moment, she sat there in silence. I continue to eat my breakfast.

"Because I'm hurt and angry, and you make me feel good," she said.

"Better than J?" I asked. I stood between her legs, grabbed her hands, and rubbed them across my stomach. Still no answer. So, I got on my knees, pulled her panties to the side, and buried my face between her thighs.

Elle

Waking up to Toni, I didn't feel any regret, but I did feel terrible and maybe a little guilty, but no regrets. I hated J, and the pain I felt in my heart wouldn't disappear. Yet, I have loved J since our first date. I reminisced as Toni ate my pussy so good.

After texting for a few days, J finally asked me on a date. I was excited that day because she took me to the Atlanta Aquarium. I was expecting dinner or maybe a walk in the park, but she surprised me when she handed me my ticket to the aquarium. I knew she had just finalized her divorce and was working crazy hours, but I was happy she had made time for me.

It was the cutest thing ever because she was so tired that day. She had just worked a big job the day before, and she was in so much pain from the rough work that when we returned to my house, I gave her a special deep massage. After, she fell into a deep sleep and didn't wake until the next day. I made sure to make her comfortable, and from that moment on, we never left each other's side.

Almost every day, J would come over after work, or I would go to her place, eat dinner, and sleep together. And when I say sleep, that's exactly what I meant because it took us a while to get physical. I wanted to wait until I knew she was over her wife before I gave her my body. I didn't want to be a rebound and fall for her too fast. Isn't that ironic?

I was wrong for popping up at her apartment, but I put so much into J. I basically nursed her back to life. I showed her how a woman is supposed to treat her lady and tried my hardest to become everything her wife wasn't. I would listen to her go on and on about her marriage as if I cared. But I only took notes of where they went wrong to know what to do right.

My feelings grew even though I knew she was still healing. I choose to invest in what we could become. So, I helped her through it as a friend. I loved her from my soul, and as far as I was concerned, she loved me too. Although she never said it. I waited patiently for the day she asked me to be her woman, but that day never came.

It was stupid popping up at her place. I just wanted to talk, but seeing who had taken her attention from me made a switch go off. Whatever her name was, she was pretty. The opposite of me, and that angered me more. The fact that they were all comfortable with their bags packed, looking like a couple going on vacation, not only put the icing on the cake but pissed me off because I never got a trip.

Now, any feelings I had for J were in the past. Fuck her. Since she was having fun and she knew about Toni and me, I figured I would have my little fun, too. Toni was sexy with street swag that matched her personality. But she wasn't like J, who took hours to get dressed and ensured everything was perfect. Toni would throw on some Tim's with her dreads hanging, a wife beater, and call it a day. Toni considered herself from the street, so she's always in the gym. J was sexy with a sexy flat stomach, but Toni's body was more masculine with a full 6-pack. Her black sports bra was covered by her dread that hung over her shoulder. Her legs were muscular, toned, and bowlegged. Last night was the first time I saw her whole body and baby, I could lick the chocolate off her skin any day. That v-cut in them guess boxers, oh baby, I couldn't take my hands off her.

Toni looked at me, looking at her body, and smiled, then buried her head back between my legs. I couldn't help but lick my lips. Replays of last night with her strapping up fucking me in every way known possible began to pop into my head. That's not including the fantastic head I was receiving at the moment.

I could deny it, Toni was sexy as fuck, and she could fuck. But I still loved J with all my heart. Even though I was hurt, I still wanted to fill her inside of me, fucking me like she loved me and didn't want anyone but me. I missed her kissing me as she moved in and out of me. I miss screaming how good she felt and how much I loved her in her ear. Still, she never said it back.

Toni was different. All my pain, all the images of the other bitch in J's room, Toni took away. She fucked the hate and worry out of me. The way Toni held me down while giving me back shot and making me submit to her when she would tell me to cum on her strap. Toni fucked me like she was making a point or proving herself. She fucked me like she wanted me, and I needed her.

"I want to smoke," I told Toni while on top of her sucking my cum off her tongue. I whipped my nut off her chin with my thumb and grabbed her face.

"Oh, so now you want to smoke. Let me find out what you are about that life," she said, gripping my ass with both hands.

"What? I'm down," I said, throwing up a fake gang sign.

"I got you, mama," she said and licked her lips. I followed her to her game room as she pulled out a little box and started to roll.

Chapter Seventeen

I woke up to my alarm and Mya lying on my chest.

"Turn it off," Mya said.

I reached over, pressed the end button, and laid back down. I wrapped my hands around her and kissed her on the forehead. As soon as I started to drift back to sleep, I felt her rubbing on my ass. Then, she kissed me on my chin while slowly working her way down my stomach with her hands. I automatically let out a moan. I don't know if it was because her hands were soft and warm or I was half unconscious, but every nerve in my body was activated, sending signals between my legs.

She pushed my legs open with her knees and climbed between them. She kissed my belly button and made slow trails with her tongue down the waistband of my briefs. I lifted my butt so that she could slide them down easily. Then, she used the tip of her fingers to spread my lips apart and kissed up and down the inside of my slit.

The sensation was more than I could handle. I could feel the wetness between my legs grow. I couldn't take the teasing anymore, so I did what the next person would do. I gripped the back of her head and fucked her face. Mya sucked on my clit like it was her last meal. Between the slurping sounds and her moans, the climax was nearing.

Before I could cum, Mya opened my legs wider and slid her fingers into my hot spot, which was now warm and wet. My body shivered as she massaged my G-spot with the tip of her fingers while softly sucking on my clit. My grip on the back of her head tightened. She was hitting all the right spots. I felt the temperature in my body rise like I was going up a mountain, and I was eager to get to the top until I climaxed on her fingers, pulling her out of me.

What was that for?" I asked her, trying to catch my breath. Instead of answering, she just kissed me. I could taste myself on her lips, which turned me on even more.

"We got to get up," she said.

"Damn, I know. Is it sad that I just want to lay here all day with you?" I said. "I know it hasn't been fifteen minutes." Mya grabbed her phone.

"Oh my god, we're so late," she said after checking the time. We both jumped up and grabbed our clothes and within fifteen minutes, we were out the door and on the road.

The ride to Myrtle Beach was perfect. Mya even loved the type of music I liked. We bumped Musiq Soulchild and Trey Songz like we were back in the early 2000s. On the way to Myrtle Beach, we stopped at a few places that caught our attention, like sex stores and fireworks spots.

For once in a long time, I was happy, even after getting a text from Elle saying, "Have fun." Nothing was going to ruin my mood. The weather was perfect, the drive was smooth, and the woman on the side of me was more beautiful than ever in her bright yellow and orange sundress. It seemed to be her favorite style. Her hair was pulled up, showing the flower tattoo on the back of her neck that I loved so much.

"You are so fucking beautiful," I said as she got comfortable. She smiled and put her hand on my thigh. I was rocking slim khaki shorts, a light blue Polo shirt, and flip-flops, looking like an American Eagle model. I finished the fit with some tan accessories Erin helped me pick out.

"We look good together," she said. I smiled and focused my attention back on the road. Around two o'clock, we arrived at the beachfront hotel.

I dropped Mya off at the lobby, parked, and grabbed our bags. By the time I got to the front door with the bags, Mya was waiting door with the keys to the room. She grabbed one of the bags hanging on my shoulders, and I followed her to the elevator.

"This is a nice hotel," I said, admiring the fancy lobby. Everything looked like it came right out of a magazine. The check-in had fish tanks built into the counter, with three flat-screen TVs behind the reception areas showing images of the rooms and pool area. There were couches in the waiting area with a flat screen over the fireplace. There even was a gift shop, and as far as I can see, they had a lot of good things in there. I made a mental note to stop by the gift shop before we left. The hotel was beautiful.

"Thanks. My mom reserved the room for us, so I knew it would be extra because she only stayed at five-star hotels," she said as we stepped onto the elevator. I put the bags down and grabbed the small of her back, bringing her closer. She let out a slight moan at my touch.

"Your mom must really like me, doesn't she?" I said, smiling.

"Yeah, surprisingly, she does. Which scares me?" Mya said.

"What does that mean?" I asked her.

"Not like that. My mom never likes anyone. She doesn't think anyone deserves me, but somehow, she loves you," she said.

"Maybe she has a reason," I said.

"That's why it scares me. I hate for my mother to be right. The whole mother-daughter rivalry is strong between us," Mya said, smiling.

"Are you going to run away from me to prove your mom wrong," I asked her, kissing her neck.

"No, I'm going to have to give her credit this time because she might be on to something," she said, pulling me closer.

"It's something about you. I don't know how we will make this work with you being so far away. But I want to try," I said. Mya kissed me on my lips, and I kissed her back. I hated the thought of her returning to Florida, but I knew she had to.

"I do, too," she whispered as the doors opened to our floor. I grabbed the bags, and she took the lead, heading towards our room door. "You know you could have let the bag boys handle our bags, right?"

"Now you tell me," I said, kicking it softly to get it back on track. Mya smiled and continued walking.

"This is it," she said as she stuck the key into the slot.

She opened the door for me. I stepped inside, and everything was white, from the living room couches to the main bedroom. Everything was white with gold trimmings. The room looked like it was built for a king.

"You like it," Mya said, grabbing my hand. I shook my head in awe. "Let's take a tour."

The king-size bed was all white and sat in the middle of the floor with gold trimmings on the pillows. The bed was so high that you had to jump up to get on it. I loved it. The elevated bed made it easier to see the ocean. I walked out to the oversized balcony, big enough to fit patio furniture and an outdoor day bed, and admired the sea. I felt like I had died and gone to heaven.

"I have never been anywhere this nice. This is how I pictured heaven to be, everything white and gold," I said.

It wasn't that I couldn't afford to stay somewhere this nice. I make over six figures a year. I just never had anyone to show me this side of life. The women I dated were cool with booking the trip through Cheaphotels.com. Hell, I was OK with it, too. But this is the next level. I was in awe.

"Originally, she was supposed to come with me, but I convinced her otherwise," she said. Mya walked over, stood behind me, and wrapped her arms around my waist.

"This hotel is crazy. I'm glad you did, and not because of the hotel but because I get a chance to get away with you and from all the drama," I said.

"Come on, it has a full bar," she said.

"Full bar, like full, like not empty," I said, like a kid in a candy store.

"Full, like unlimited. Drink whatever because it's on my mom's tab and not mine," she said. We both burst out laughing.

She led me to the mini bar and opened it. It was filled with shots of all kinds of alcohol. On the top of the counter was a bucket of ice, a bottle of wine, and a note.

"Congratulations, Mya. You're going to do great—love Coach. Thanks, Coach," she said, reading the card and placing it back next to the bottle.

"Everyone is so happy for you. I know your mom must feel proud," I say, grabbing and opening two shots of vodka. I handed one to Mya, and we took the shot to the head together.

"Yeah, she wasn't supportive at first. But ever since my father passed, she just wanted to be a part of everything in my life. Now, I think she is more excited about this wedding than I am," she said, grabbing more shots. "Let's head out to the beach for a while. I have to meet the family at eight for the rehearsal dinner."

"I'm already ahead of you," I said, ripping open my suitcase and grabbing a pair of swimming trunks. I was beyond ready to relax by the beach with this beautiful woman.

After getting dressed, we walked to the surf shop across from the hotel. We bought beach blankets, a cooler, sunscreen, snacks, and an umbrella to protect us from the sun. Once we got everything, we headed to the beach.

We spent the rest of the afternoon running from the water to our beach towels. We would play in the water for a while, cuddle on the blanket, talk until we dried off, and then repeat the process. It was the perfect afternoon.

"So, what are your plans when you get back to Florida?" I said, sitting on a beach towel with my head resting between Mya's legs.

"I don't know, school hasn't started back, but probably clean my apartment. Do you know that I leave as soon as we get back? I think my plane takes off early the next morning," she said.

"You're leaving me that fast?" I said. I grabbed and kissed the back of her hand.

"Yeah, I don't want to, but I gotta," she said, placing a soft kiss on the top of my head.

"Listen, let's just enjoy today. I don't want to think about you leaving right now," I said

"Yeah, you're right. Let's enjoy the moment," Mya said, gazing at the beach. She wrapped her arms around my neck and kissed my forehead. She rested her chin on my head, and we both watched and listened to the ocean, lost in our thoughts.

"What are you thinking about?" I said, breaking the silence.

"Honestly?" Mya asked.

"Yeah, honestly."

"I want to tell you something, but I'm scared. I also want to protect you, and that may mean me telling you," Mya said.

"Okay, enough with the riddles. Just talk to me," I said.

"I know we haven't been seeing each other long, but I feel like I know everything about you or enough to know that I like you a lot."

"And I like you too," I said.

"Since the park, I had been receiving death threats from Drea," she said.

"Death threats? Why haven't you said anything?" I said, leaning up and facing her. Tears began to run down her face.

"She's been sending me crazy emails threatening us both.," she said.

"Wow! What exactly do the emails say?" I said.

"A lot of curse words and harming us both if she sees us again. Threatening me if I don't leave you alone. Saying crazy things like she owns me. She doesn't know where I live or my mother, so I didn't take it seriously, but when she mentioned you, that scared me," she said.

"No one is going to hurt me. You are safe. I won't let anyone hurt you, either," I said.

"Who is your favorite actor?" Mya asked, changing the subject.

"I'll watch anything with Will Smith. Just name it. I love it," I said.

"What's your favorite Will Smith movie?" Mya asked me.

"All the bad boys," I said, laughing.

For the rest of our time on the beach, we sat chatting for what seemed like hours, asking each other different questions about our future and dreams and avoiding questions about our past.

"It's getting late. I still need to get changed. We both do. That rehearsal starts in a few," she said as the sun faded.

"Yeah, I'm ready to get this sand off me," I said.

We packed everything and headed back to the hotel. When we returned, we showered together to wash the sand from us and quickly got dressed. I looked sexy in my slim khakis and a white button-up. I pulled my hair back into a curly bun and was ready to go.

It took Mya a little longer. Eventually, she was ready. She wore a light blue sundress that wrapped around her neck. I helped her pack her equipment and headed to the rehearsal dinner. Luckily, the rehearsal was a few hotels down because we were almost running late.

The rehearsal dinner was great. Even though Mya was working, everyone treated me like I was family. I was laughing and joking with everyone all evening. Now and then, Mya and I would sneak a few glances at each other, blowing air kisses in between her snapping photos. The young couple that was getting married was adorable. They seemed excited and so in love. I couldn't help but want that, too. Maybe, one day, with Mya.

Mya was walking around taking pictures when she saw me dancing with some random guy. We were both drunk and having a great time playfully jumping around the dance floor. Mya started snapping photos of us. We stopped dancing and started posing as if we were at a photoshoot. Mya couldn't stop laughing.

"Give me that camera and dance with her," the bride-to-be told Mya. "You've taken enough pictures and videos. Go enjoy yourself."

"Yeah, you're officially off. Everyone is starting to leave anyway," the groom said, joining in and hugging his wife-to-be from behind.

"Thanks," Mya said, giving them a friendly smile.

I pretended to fish, throwing the line to Mya and winding my hands like I caught a big one. She shook her head, laughed, and danced over to me.

"You are having too much fun without me," she said, wrapping her arms around my head.

"These my people. I was waiting for you. Are you ready to get out of here? I want to walk on the beach."

"Yeah," she said. She stared into my eyes, focusing on each pupil, then kissed me softly. I held her tight and picked her up off the ground, spinning her to the sound of the music. The bride-to-be began snapping pictures of us with Mya's camera. The moment was perfect.

Elle

Many may wonder what I'm doing chasing after this young ass girl, but J is the most mature and financially secure masculine presenting female I've run into. I have been in many relationships, with my longest lasting almost ten years. During those ten years, I've dealt with cheating and mental, emotional, and physical abuse. I've been homeless, living on friend couches, and struggling even to afford a bus pass.

Most of the bad things that happened in my life were due to me following behind some no-good studs. I have been a lesbian my whole life, never even dealing with a man. To all my straight friends thinking women are easier, I'm here to tell her that's a damn lie. My only downfall is I fall in love easily and love too hard.

It wasn't until I was in my late thirties that I found my dream job and have been able to afford the lifestyle I live now. When I met J, I was looking for someone with the same financial status as me, and I found that in her. She knew and understood my insecurities, and I know I may go overboard at times, but my worst fear is that someone will see what I see and take her from me. She's the best thing I've had, but I messed that all up.

I ended up staying for a while smoking and fucking with Toni. I texted J earlier and told her and that bitch to have fun. I knew she wouldn't respond, but it was worth a try, and I felt better. I can't stop talking about how J and I reached this point, and I know it was aggravating Toni.

Toni has always been jealous of J. Everyone can see that, but I never understood why. From the stories J told me, I wonder if she's still friends with her, but that was never my place to judge. I would listen to J complain, rub her head, and tell her to watch her back. But, of course, it was something she already knew.

All I wanted to do was know where things were heading with J and me, and in less than a week, we'd broken up from whatever I thought we had; J was flaunting around a new chick, and I slept with her best friend. So, how did we get to this point?

I guess I'm just hurt it happened. Regardless of what everybody may think, I'm in love with J. She was the first woman who was nice and treated me the way I always dreamed. All I wanted was a laid-back woman who had her own shit and treated me well. Don't get me wrong, J and I had our issues, but she's a good woman, and all I wanted was some clarity as to what I did wrong. It doesn't matter now.

After this little stunt with Toni, I know the chances of us getting back together were slim to none. But I'll be damned if I let that bitch have her. I knew I was wrong, but sleeping with Toni made me forget about everything, and she made me feel so good and took away this pain in my chest. The way Toni fucks, she can take away my pain anytime. I closed my legs, replaying last night, still feeling her 9-inch strap inside me.

I pulled up to my apartment around four o'clock. I needed to rest. I was tired, and Toni wore me out to the fullest. Also, her 9-inch friend had me a little sore between the legs. It had been a while since J and I had done anything like that, so my little cat was damn near a virgin.

I opened my door and landed right on the couch. Immediately, my body relaxed as I reached for the remote and turned on the TV. When I got comfortable, my phone went off, letting me know it was a text message. I reached and grabbed it from the table.

Toni: I just wanted to make sure.
you've made it home alright.

Although I should have been sleeping, I decided to text her back. Fuck it, J was out with her new flunky, so I might as well stay entertained.

Me: Yeah, I just laid down on the couch.
Are you missing me already?

Toni: I mean, the way this morning
has gone, who wouldn't miss you?
I wish you wouldn't have left so soon.

Me: Yeah, I knew you wanted me to stay,
but I don't want things to get out of hand.
We both know what this is.

I didn't want Toni to get into her feelings. I had known her long enough to see that she was jealous of J. Anyone who has been around them long enough can tell that. I didn't want her to get the wrong idea. She is a good fuck, but that's all.

Toni: I know the game, man. I invented it.
Whenever you need to talk again, just hit me up.

Me: I may need to "talk" later tonight.
You know us girls always got something
on your mind.

Toni: I'm here to listen. Oh, and bring a change of clothes. I got a quick errand to run tonight, but I should be back early enough to tap that ass tonight and tomorrow morning. So, you're going to need a few showers when I'm done with you.

Me: Yes, sir.

I can't lie. Toni's sex is addictive. But she is not the type of girl you bring home to Mom. The fact that she only talks to hood females shows a lot about her character. Even though she had a good job, you would never know because she carried herself like she was still in the streets. But the girl can fuck, and I can see why she always has drama. Just the thought started to turn me on. She got the kind of sex that will make bitches go crazy. Hell, she has me running back for more.

Chapter Eighteen

After the rehearsal, we decided to walk to the hotel. It was a little after midnight, and night was still young. The moon was bright in the sky. We packed all her equipment, locked the car doors, and walked along the beach, watching the waves crash into the deserted shore.

"I had a really good time," I said to Mya.

"I'm glad you did. For a minute, it seemed like you were a part of the wedding and forgot about me," Mya said.

"They made me feel comfortable. I felt like I was. Let's sit for a minute," I said, grabbing Mya's hand and leading her to an empty beach chair. She sat in between my legs, facing the ocean.

"It's pretty dark out here," she said.

"Yeah, but there's a couple over there," I said, pointing at the men and women lying together on the lawn chair.

"Oh, okay! I feel better," she said.

"I told you. I got you. I know we've talked about you leaving and us saying goodbye, but have you ever thought about whether we could work?" I said.

"Yes, But I'm just scared to go there with you," Mya said.

"Why?" I asked her, staring into the dark ocean. I grabbed her hand and placed it in mine.

"It's a lot going on, and I don't want to bring you into my drama," she said.

"We already admitted that we both have drama but are still here. Is it because of the emails?" I said.

"Have you thought about it?" she asked.

"The email? Or us?" I ask.

"Us."

"Yes, of course. All the time," I said.

"And? Do you think we could work?" Mya said.

Would it work? I don't know. I've never been in a long-distance relationship. Mya was halfway through graduate school, and my business was in Atlanta. Would we have time to explore a relationship? I wanted to tell Mya I was falling in love with her, but I was scared it was too soon. I was also afraid that she wouldn't feel the same way. I turned her towards me, wrapped her legs around my waist, and pulled her closer.

"Yeah, I want to try," I told her honestly. Mya grabbed my face and looked into my eyes as if she was trying to find the truth.

"I do, too," she said, wrapping her arms around my neck. I pulled her into a tight hug. I grabbed my phone and took a picture of us. I posted it on Twitter with a caption: Enjoying myself with this beauty.

Toni

I was playing video games when I heard a knock on the door. I knew it was Elle because she had texted me about an hour earlier to tell me she was on the way. I climbed out of my chair and headed to the door. I was happy that she had finally gotten here because, after sexting all day, I needed to feel her body.

When I opened the door, Elle wore a black robe like a good girl. I had told her to come naked, but I didn't think she would. I pulled her to the door, closed it behind her, and slowly opened her robe. She wore a red, laced bra and panty set. I licked my lips and led her into the bedroom. Elle grabbed my stash and began rolling up.

"You got something to drink?" Elle asked.

"Hell yeah. I'll make some shots," I said. When I walked back to the room, Elle was drying to blunt. When she was done, she slowly undid her robe.

"I didn't think you would do it," I said, handing her a shot. We both took them to the head. I grabbed her glass and set them both on the dresser.

"What can I say? You have a way of persuading women to do what you want," she said seductively.

I opened Elle's robe and slowly pushed her to the bed. I got on my knees, pulled down her panties to the side, and buried my face between her legs. Elle lifted her legs, spreading them wide, and gripped the back of my head. Elle fucked my face as I struggled to breathe between licks. I reached over and grabbed my strap from the bag under the bed. I slipped on the 9-inch without missing a beat.

I stood up, spit into my hand, and rubbed it up and down the shaft. Spreading Elle's legs wider, I slowly slide inside of her. Elle took a deep breath, arched her back, and pulled me closer to her.

For the next few hours, I had Elle in every position I could think of, and after she came multiple times, she pushed me down on the bed, spread, and climbed between my legs.

"What are you doing, Elle?" I said while she aggressively undid my strap and pulled my underwear down.

"Please, let me please you," she said.

I had always been a pleaser, a touch-me-not if you want to put a label on it, but the way Elle licked her lips as she slowly ran her soft hands up my legs had my shit jumping. Elle guided me to the edge of the bed and got down on her knees.

For the first time in over ten years, I allowed her to do something only my first girlfriend had done to me. Give me head.

I held on to the back of Elle's head as she licked and slurped my clit. The way her head bounced up and down as if she was deep-throating my shit had my toes curling. Elle treated my clit like she knew what she was doing and had me moaning shit like "suck it" as I helped her head bounce, only to stop when I came into her mouth.

When she was done, she licked her lips and wiped my nut from the corners of her mouth with her thumb. I leaned back onto my hands and stared at the ceiling, smiling at the thought of having J's woman on her knees sucking up my nut.

"What are you smiling like that for? You like that?" Elle said, pushing my forehead back, climbing on top, and straddling me.

"I like that a lot. But don't get used to that shit," I said, gripping her ass and digging three fingers into her pussy. Elle ran her fingers up my back, gripping the back of my locs. I slide my fingers deeper inside, massaging her walls and exploring every ripple of her tunnel.

I knew Elle was using me and understood her reason for it. She was hurt, but J didn't deserve Elle. She needed to know and feel that. I could give Elle everything plus more than what J could ever provide. I could fuck her in ways J had never dreamed of.

With free hand, I gripped Elle's lower back, pulling her closer to me. Elle began rotating her hips, moaning loudly. After another round, Elle collapsed on my chest.

"Oh my gosh," Elle said, breathing into my neck.

"Damn, girl," I said, moving her to the side and placing her leg on top of me. Elle had my ass butt naked, laid across her bed. No sports bra, socks, or anything.

"You know you can fuck?" Elle said, rotating her fingers around my nipple.

"I know. I get a lot of compliments." Elle squeezed my nipple hard. "What the fuck?" I said, grabbing my little chest.

"You play too much. I don't want to picture you sleeping with someone else. Leave the details to yourself," Elle said.

"I don't need to tell you the details. I can show you," I said, climbing on top of Elle. Elle is amazing, but she needs a real woman like me to show her that. J couldn't handle a woman like Elle.

Eventually Elle passed out. I wanted to stay and hold her all night, but after Elle passed out, my phone began to vibrate on the nightstand. It was a text from my bro.

Bro: Are you ready?

Me: Yeah, be done in 10.

I know I had made plans with Elle, but these plans were already made before sexting led here to my front door. I had promised to ride with my stud bro that night.

Ten minutes later, I was out the door and in my truck in all black to blend in with the night. I hopped in my brother's truck, and he immediately pulled off. I knew that Elle wouldn't wake up any time soon because I crushed up some sleeping pills and added them to the shot we downed somewhere between round two or three. I needed Elle to think we passed out together.

Once we got to the destination, he pulled up to the back of another car and turned off the headlights. We got out of the car and hopped in the other.

"So, what happens now?" I asked as she handed me a blunt. I lit it and passed it to my brother.

"Just ride, bro!" Drea said and pulled off.

J

I woke up the following day with Mya cuddled next to me. I couldn't stop thinking about her ex and everything she told me. She seemed scared last night, and I barely slept because I needed to know more. I had a lot of questions on my mind, but I didn't think she was ready to answer them. I placed soft kisses on Mya's forehead.

"What time is it?" she said, kissing the bottom of my chin.

"Good morning, beautiful. It's still early," I told Mya, pulling her closer to me.

"Why are you awake?"

"I don't know. I guess I have a lot on my mind," I said.

"What's on your mind?" Mya said.

It took me a minute to answer her question. I wanted to ask her about Drea's emails. I wanted to talk about our future relationship. I wanted to tell her how I felt.

"I'm going to miss you," I said instead. I didn't want to ruin the moment.

"I'll be back to visit you. You can always come to visit me. This doesn't have to end here," she said.

The vibration of her phone scared us both. She grabbed her phone, sighed, got up, and grabbed the robe the hotel provided. Mya walked to the bathroom. When she closed the door, I rolled over and got my phone. I had one missed call from Erin. I pressed send and put the phone to my ear. She answered on the third ring.

"You need to leave your girl alone," Erin said immediately.

"What are you talking about? What girl? And good morning to you, too," I said, laughing.

"Toni..." she started to say before Mya walked out of the bathroom. I immediately turned my attention to her. Mya's eyes were puffy, like she had been crying.

"Let me call you back," I told Erin, hanging up. I jumped up and ran towards Mya, who fell into my arms and began to cry. "Mya, what's wrong?"

"We got to go," she said between sobs.

"Okay, I'll get the bags," I said. I grabbed my suitcase and began to throw clothes inside quickly. Mya did the same, still quietly sobbing.

"We have to hurry?" Mya said.

"Can you just tell me what's wrong? What about the wedding?" I said, grabbing the rest of my things.

"I'll tell you in the car. I can get the wedding covered, but I need to get back home now," she said.

"Fuck, the truck. I'll be back. I'm going to go get my truck," I said. I had forgotten that we had walked back to the hotel last night.

"Okay, just hurry back," Mya said as I exited the room.

As soon as I got out of the hotel, I called Erin. She picked up on the first ring.

"Hey, Erin. What's up? I asked her.

"You need to leave your friend alone. Like seriously," she said.

"Erin, who? I don't have time for this," I said as I began to pick up the pace. I needed to get my truck and get back to Mya to see what was happening.

"Toni. She's up to no good, and I don't trust her. You need to be careful," Erin said.

"Erin, I don't trust Toni either. But I gotta go," I said, almost running at full speed. Once I reached my truck, I hopped in quickly and drove back to the hotel. I pulled up to the hotel, and Mya stood outside the hotel with all our belongings sitting at her feet. Once we got everything packed, we hopped on the highway.

Chapter Nineteen

On the drive back to Atlanta, Mya sat in the passenger seat with her phone glued to her hand. She had been on the phone with her mom all morning because someone had broken into her home, damaged it, and stolen most of her valuable items. From what I had overheard, her mom was at the house with the police, going over missing items. Mya had already called a locksmith to change the locks, and he was on the way. Mya's phone vibrated again in her hand. She unlocked it, glanced at the notification, then placed her phone in her lap.

"I'm sorry. This vacation didn't quite turn out how I planned," Mya said.

I placed one hand on her thigh and gave her a small smile while still trying to keep my eyes on the road.

"Don't apologize, Mya. I'm sorry this happened to you and your mom. I'm just happy that I am here, and you were here with me and not there," I said, grabbing her hand and kissing it. She smiled, relaxed, and put her phone in the cup holder.

Five hours later, I pulled up into Mya's mom's driveway. Before I could come to a complete stop, she jumped out and ran into the house, calling for her mom. I parked quickly and followed her. As we ran through the front door, I heard her mom say she was in the kitchen.

Mya started crying as we walked through her childhood home. The nicely decorated home was now filled with pieces of glass from the broken tables. The sofa sliced as if someone took a knife and walked along the back, digging deep into the fabric. Everything in the home was either broken, damaged, or ripped.

Mya's room was the worst. Her clothes were everywhere, her bed sheets were ripped, television was smashed, but what freaked me out was her panties were in a pile placed neatly on the bed as if someone took their time and folded them. This robbery was personal.

"Who would do this?" Mya's mom asked, coming behind us as we stood in the doorway of Mya's room. Mya turned around and hugged her mom. She sobbed quietly in her arms.

"We need to leave. The police will do whatever they can to find out who did this, but right now, let's get you guys out of here. It's been a long day, and we can all use some rest," I said.

"Janice is right, mom. Let's go to my hotel. You can't stay here tonight." Mya said.

"Fine," Mrs. Autumn said.

The police were gone, the locks had been changed, and the sun was starting to set. The way the house looked, there was no way they could have stayed there.

"Come on. I'll take you. Neither one of you should drive right now," I said.

"No, you've done enough. Go home and get some rest," Mya said.

"How can I sleep right now?" I said.

"There is nothing you can do. Why stay?" Mya said.

"Mya. If you think I'm leaving you, you must be crazy. We both know why," I said, remembering the threatening emails from her ex. Mya told her mom to get some stuff and meet her at the car. She grabbed my hand and led me to the front door.

"J, thank you, but you've done enough," she said as she opened the door.

"I don't want to leave you right now. I don't think this was a random robbery," I told Mya.

"I think Drea did this," Mya said. I looked down at her and saw the tears forming in her eyes.

"I figured as much. This was personal, and if you think I'm leaving you alone, you don't know me at all," I said, hugging her tight. I didn't want to let her go. I wanted to protect her forever.

"I know, but I have to take care of my mom. I'll call you tonight," she said, wrapping her hands around my waist. I kissed her on her forehead.

"You sure you don't want me to drive you?" I asked her one last time.

"Yeah, I'm going to take her to my hotel. She needs to rest. We all need some rest," she said.

"I don't like it, but I guess I have no choice," I said, pulling her close. "If you need me, call me." I grabbed her face and kissed her softly on her lips. She kissed me back and wrapped her arms around my neck.

"Why does she keep torturing me? I moved out of state. I changed my number. Why won't she leave me alone?" she asked, buried between my head and shoulder.

"I don't know, baby. I don't care what you say. You're riding with me. I'm going to drop you and Mom off at your hotel, run home, and grab a few things," I said. "Go help your mom. I'll be in the car."

She just nodded and walked back into the house. Ten minutes later, Mya and Mrs. Autumn left their home, holding a duffle bag. I hopped out of my truck and helped them both into the car.

"Do you mind dropping my mom off at her friends' house?" Mya said.

"Of course," I said as we pulled off. After dropping Mrs. Autumn off, we drove quietly back to Mya's hotel.

"I'm sorry for putting you through this. I didn't mean to add you to my drama," she said as we pulled into the hotel.

"It's all right. I'm going to ride with you through all of this. I'm a big girl. I can make my own decision, but I thought we agreed to stop apologizing for our exes," I said, trying to lighten the mood. Mya giggled and grabbed my hand.

"Thank you," she said.

"Your mom has insurance, right?" I asked.

"Yeah, she's not worried about the material stuff. It's just the fact that someone came into her home. I can't tell her I believe Drea had something to do with it. But I know it was her," she said.

"I figured. But why are you so sure?" I asked.

"She broke into my apartment before during one of the millions of times we broke up. One day, I came home to everything destroyed but my panties, which were folded neatly on the bed," she said and lowered her head.

"That's some creepy, stalker shit."

"I should have known something wasn't right with her then. Her excuse was that she thought I was sleeping with someone else."

"And you took her back?"

"I didn't have a choice. She was crying about being hungry and sleeping in her car. I couldn't watch her suffer. Things got a lot worse after that. It was like I was trapped. I couldn't get away from her. If I tried, she ruined everything around me. It was easier to stay," she said.

"As long as you're with me, I promise I won't let anything happen to you," I said.

Once we got to the hotel, I helped her carry her bags to her room and around to ensure she was safe.

"Look, I have to run home really quick. I need to grab and check on some things, but don't open this door for anyone, only me," I told Mya.

"How long are you going to be gone?" Mya asked.

"I will call you when I'm heading up, maybe an hour," I told her. I grabbed and held her tight.

"Hurry back. Please, and be careful," she said, grabbing my shirt and pulling me closer. I kiss her on the forehead before breaking our hold.

"I will. I love you," I said, not realizing the words that came from my mouth.

"I love you too," she said. I pulled her face up to mine and kissed her on the lips. Everything in me told me to stay, but I had no clean clothes besides dress clothes that were supposed to be for the wedding. We were leaving immediately after, so I didn't pack any extra. After today's events, I just wanted to shower and hold Mya all night.

"I'll be back," I said, walking out the door.

I jumped in my truck and searched for my phone. I was in trouble and didn't know what I had gotten into. I wanted to call Toni, but I knew she was sleeping with Elle, and I couldn't handle that right now. I was scared for Mya and her mom, and I just wanted to protect them, but I didn't know where to start. I felt lost. I dialed the only other person I knew.

"Come on, Erin. Pick up!" I said out loud. It was only 9:30, so I knew she should have been up. After a minute or so, her voicemail came on. FUCK! I said, hitting the steering wheel.

Me: Hey, I'm heading to Mya's hotel. She ran into some shit with her ex, and the bitch is psycho, and I mean restraining order crazy. Call me back!

I didn't know who else to call, and with Mya so scared and shaken up, I didn't know what Drea was capable of. I needed to vent or at least tell someone what was going on. Against my better judgment, I decided to call Toni. After all, she is usually the first person I call during times like this. I still don't know what's going on with her, but that would be a conversation for another day. We've fallen out many times before, but I needed her now more than ever.

"What's up, Toni? What you up to?" I said, feeling dumb as hell, but I didn't know who else to call. All I could think about was Mya, and I'd do anything for her. This was a crazy situation. If anybody knew what to do, Toni would.

"Well damn! Look who it is! What's up? I heard you went out of town?" Toni said.

"Yeah, I needed to clear my head," I said.

"Is that so? So, what are you calling me for?" she asked.

"I wouldn't call you if I didn't need you," I began but stopped. "Look, Toni. Someone broke into Mya's mom's house..."

"And!" She said, cutting me off and laughing. "What that got to do with me?"

"That's what we do know? "I asked.

"Aye, look, I'm going to call you back. I got somebody. I meant something to do. It seems like you got your hands full. I'm sure it's a lot of cleaning up to do?" Toni said and hung up. I called her back about five times and got the voicemail.

What did she mean by "cleaning up"? I never told her exactly what happened. I needed clarification. Did she have something to do with it? I didn't know what was happening, so I hopped on the highway. I swear if she had something to do with this, I was going to kill her ass! I hopped on the highway and drove straight to Toni's. I called Mya to check on her.

"Hey, baby. Are you ok?" I asked her.

"Yeah, I'm just tired. I'm about to shower and get in bed. Can you hurry back, please?" Mya said.

"Yeah, I need to check on something. I promise I will be back. Just ensure the bolt lock is on before jumping in the shower." I said.

"Ok, just hurry up," she said.

"I will," I said and hung up the phone.

I went to Toni's apartment in record time, ran up the stairs, and knocked on the door. I could hear her footsteps through the door.

"Who is it?" Toni yelled.

"It's me. Toni, open the door!" I yelled back. I heard her unlocking the locks and laughing.

"So, what brings you to my side of town?" Toni asked, trying to be funny. I ignored her question and walked through the door. I needed to know what she meant. I needed answers quickly so I could get back to Mya.

"How did you know Mya's house got trashed?" I asked, getting to the point. She laughed, which just made me even more angry.

"It's a small world. You think you know everything, but you don't know shit. You didn't know Mya had a girl while you were there acting like she was all yours. She's playing your dumb ass," Toni said.

'What are you talking about?"

"I knew that I knew Mya from somewhere. I just couldn't put my finger on it. Her girl, Drea! Yeah, that's my cousin. If I were you, I would stay away from her. Drea isn't happy about what you and Mya got going on," she said with a smile. Every word from her mouth made me want to choke her.

As soon as I was about to respond, the bedroom door opened, and Elle walked out with a devious grin. I almost didn't recognize her. Her hair was wild, her clothes barely on, and her eyes were bloodshot red. I knew she was high. I couldn't help but laugh. Both were standing there looking like the devil and his pawn. I almost felt sorry for her. *Ain't this a Bitch!*

"Babe, go back in the room," Toni told her. Hearing her say that made my skin crawl. Elle walked back into the bedroom, and Toni just stood there smiling.

"I knew you were shady. I just never believed that you were that evil," I told Toni, staring dead into her eyes. I clenched my fist so tight it felt like my nails were digging into the palms of my hands.

"Man, whatever you need to stop worrying about us and go check on your bitch. Last I heard, you walked her to her room carrying her bags. I think Drea wants her girlfriend back," she said, grinning.

The thought of Mya just made me break. I stepped over and swung with everything I had: pain, hurt, and betrayal all came out in a mighty blow, knocking Toni off her feet. She hit her head on the corner of the door and fell to the floor. I got on top of her and was sending blows left and right. All I could hear was her next-door neighbor walking out her front door, screaming that we were fighting.

I felt someone pull me off Toni and roughly push me into the door. I tried to run back to Toni, but the same hands grabbed me and carried me down the stairs. It wasn't until I was halfway to the parking lot that I realized I wasn't getting any closer to her.

"Calm the fuck down!" A deep voice said.

"Let go of me," I said, snatching away.

"You need to get out of here before somebody calls the police, and then we're going to have a problem," he said, pushing me into the parking lot. "Get the fuck out of here!"

I could hear Toni in the background laughing. I glanced up at the top of the stairs and saw Elle nursing Toni's wounds on the balcony. I shook my head, got in the car, and drove off. I grabbed my phone and had eleven missed calls and one voicemail. All the missed calls were from Mya. Fuck Fuck Fuck. I grabbed my phone and called her back. No answer. I called again, voicemail. I called again, but nothing.

I threw my phone in the passenger seat before remembering having a voicemail. I picked it back up. It was Mya. She said someone was banging on the door, and then the phone hung up. I called Mya again,... no answer. I started to panic and pushed on the gas. I needed to get to her. I called Erin again, and this time she picked up.

"Hey, what's going on? I just got out of the movies," Erin said.

"Somethings wrong. I think Toni broke into Mya's house while we were gone. I know she had something to do with it, and I believe the ex is at her hotel now. I need you to meet me." I said.

"Do I need to call the police?" she asked.

"Yes, that is probably a good idea. Just hurry up and meet me, ok? Toni and I got into a fight. I snapped when I saw Elle come out of her room." I said. I hated myself for going there with her, especially since Mya was in trouble.

"I knew it! Elle has been acting strange for the last few days. That's what I wanted to call you about earlier. I told you I didn't trust Toni. I'm on the way. Text me the address," she said. Her voice told me that she was either walking fast or running.

"Fuck Elle and Fuck Toni, too. Erin, I don't know what to do if something happens to Mya," I said, trying to hold back the tears.

"I'm on the way!" she said and hung up. I immediately texted her the address of Mya Hotel.

Ten minutes later, I pulled up her hotel, hopped out, and handed my keys to the valet. I ran inside, not even giving him my information. I ran up the stairs, skipping every other one. I reached her door and put my key into the slot. I could hear her yelling through the door. I slid the key into the lock, but the light on the keypad would not turn green. I tried again and again. I could hear Mya yelling stop hurting me. I couldn't get through. After about fifteen tries, the door finally opened.

I ran through the door and to her room. I could hear Mya screaming for help. I got to the door, and it was locked. I banged on the door and told her to open it.

"Is that the bitch, huh?" I heard Drea say. Mya screamed. I tried to break through the door but couldn't get through.

"Let her go," I screamed through the door, banging as hard as possible.

"I told you that you're mine, bitch! The bitch can't save you." I heard her say, followed by a loud slap and thump. I kicked and kicked the door. It wouldn't budge. I started screaming Mya's name. I could hear her crying, telling Drea to stop. I heard Drea yelling words that weren't making sense. "If I can't have you, she won't either," was all I could make out.

I heard a gun cock and Mya scream. With everything in me, I kicked the door, which flew open. The sight of Mya balled up in the corned bleeding and Drea standing over her with a gun in her hand made me swing into action. I began to run towards Drea.

BOOM!

My heart dropped as I saw Mya's body jerk and hit the wall. I grabbed Drea and swung her across the room as hard as I could. The gun dropped out of her hand as she crashed into the hanging wall mirror. I grabbed the gun and ran over to Mya. Her body was limp, and blood was everywhere, but I could hear her breathing.

"Baby, Baby, stay with me," I said. I dropped the gun and began applying pressure to the bullet wound in Mya's stomach.

When I turned around, Drea stood over me with the gun in her hand. I pleaded with Drea while I held onto Mya. I couldn't feel Mya breathing anymore.

"Baby, hold on for me. Please," I cried.

Drea stood over me, looking down with a devilish smirk that would make the strongest man fear for his life. Her eyes were empty and full of hatred. I did the only thing I could. I clutched onto Mya and closed my eyes.

BOOM!

Chapter Twenty:
Two years later

"You are the light, my love, and my everything. I love you more than life itself. Through everything you've been through, you never stopped smiling. You are the strongest woman I know. Amya Shanell Autumn, will you marry me?" I asked on one knee.

"Yes, yes, yes!" Mya said as tears fell from her face. I slid the ring on her finger and got back up. She wrapped her arms around my neck and kissed me deeply.

There we were, two years later, back at Myrtle Beach. I brought her back to where I first realized I had fallen in love with her. It's the true start of our love story. I never in a million years thought that we would be here. But here we were.

That day, I thought that I lost her. I thought I was dead, too. But the police busted through the door just as she was about to pull the trigger and shot her right between the eyes. Mya made it out ok. She lost a lot of blood and had to stay in the hospital for a while, but I was there through every step. If I wasn't there, her mom was. I would stay overnight and lay on the small couch beside her bed. I only left long enough to shower and change clothes.

I helped her mom sold and move to a different house where she felt safe and secure. Mya was released from the hospital two weeks later. It took her a while to recover after taking a bullet to the stomach. But my baby was strong. I knew she would pull through.

She stayed at my house for about a month while she continued to heal, and then I packed up everything and moved down to Florida with her while she finished school. There was nothing for me in Atlanta anymore but bad memories. I still work in construction and was taking the new city by storm.

After she graduated, Mya focused full-time on her photography. Although her mom and I thought she should take a break from school, she was adamant about finishing. She said she did it for her father. Since then, Mya has been freelancing, making good money, booking weddings, baby showers, etc.

I bet you are wondering what happened to Toni. Well, let's say she's not the most intelligent burglar.

Her face was all over the security cameras in the home and the entrance to the subdivision. They arrested her and her brother the day after the shooting, seeing them on camera with Drea. They both were found guilty, and Toni received ten years in prison while her brother received fifteen.

She and her brother had been doing this for a while with our old clients. They waited months after a project and broke into the customer's homes. With the time difference, the owners never expected a thing. I'm glad it caught up with her. I had to change my company's name and everything else to protect my brand. I had to start from scratch, but I hired workers instead of doing it myself. So far, I had three overworked employees and plan on expanding soon.

The last I heard of Elle, she got drunk at the bar she loved so much and caused a fight. According to Erin, they banned her. Other than that, nothing has changed with her. Erin used to keep me updated, but after Elle had gotten into a relationship, I told her to stop. I hope she finds someone to love her. All that is in the past now. I'm getting married!

"I love you, Janice," she said, grabbing my hands and pulling them around her. I kissed her on her neck and pulled her close.

"I love you too," I said.

****Leave your feedback with the hashtag #Studbrosthebook on TikTok and follow the author @SJthewriter for a chance to win a FREE autographed hard copy****

About the Author

S.J. Mitch founded Written Creativity, an online platform dedicated to helping new and seasoned writers sell their manuscripts. S.J. holds a bachelor's degree in creative writing and a double master's in Entertainment

Business and Digital Marketing. She is also a freelance writer and editor and has multiple short stories published in popular literacy magazines like The Scarlet Leaf Review. You can find her on all social media apps under the name @SJThewriter.

DON'T FORGET TO LEAVE A REVIEW!

Made in the USA
Columbia, SC
10 February 2024

31144069R00171